Everything Works Out In The End

MARWA CHAMI

INDIA • SINGAPORE • MALAYSIA

ISBN 979-8-89544-546-4

For all the girls who experienced their first love in high school.

(And for anyone who's living an unfair life),

Playlist

Summertime Sadness

Lana Del Rey

Love In the Dark

Adele

A Drop in the Ocean

Ron Pope

Wings

Birdy

A Sky Full of Stars

Coldplay

Je te laisserai des mots.

Patrick Watson

Everything Works Out in the End

Kodaline

Content notes

This story contains inappropriate language and topics that may be sensitive to some readers.

Readers aged 15 and over are eligible to read this story.

Everything

Works Out

In The End

Contents

Chapter 1
Avène

"June 17th, at our favourite mojito place."

"I know, this is the 5th time you've repeated this," Alex returned as he opened Instagram on his new iPhone 15, which he had been bragging about. "By the way, why did you choose to celebrate your 21st birthday at a mojito place while inviting *your CRUSH*?"

"I love the way they treat the mojitos like a piece of art, and I'm inviting him because I want to recreate that day." On June 17th, seven years ago, I invited this same guy to my 14th birthday party. It was fun, but three days after that day, I found myself in chaos.

"You want to recreate that day? Are you sure about that? I mean, you went through a lot, and it's been five years since you two started talking again, which is good, but it's your golden birthday. *EVERYTHING* must be perfect," Alex said as he looked away from his phone, looking like he was searching for a hint of sorrow that could still be in me from that day.

"I'm an adult now. I can handle this, don't worry. I know it's cool that I was born on June 21, 2003, at 9:06 pm, with my age soon-to-be 21. I know it must be a perfect party with only *smiles.* And to be honest, I'm scared, but time changes people. I want to give him a chance. I want to know if he truly cares about all those mixed signals he has been giving me for five years now. Alex, I can't move on if I don't get my closure. I'm desperate. It's been seven years..."

I kept on rambling all my feelings to Alex. As he came to me for our traditional comfort hug, my phone's screen lit up. It's the message I've been waiting for.

Nicholas.

"I'm outside," was the one and only message he sent with no heads up. We haven't spoken since Tuesday *last week.* How can he just show up? I don't even know if I look good after the crying session I just had with Alex. But before I knew it, Nicholas came in and stood right beside me.

"Hi, Avène," is that all he's going to say?

"Hi, Nicholas." This is awkward. He always does this. "I want to talk to you. Alone," he said while looking at Alex with envy burning behind those beautiful, fiery hazel eyes.

I look up to Alex to get his approval. To follow Nicholas, he nodded. That one nod had an entire sentence behind it. *Go ahead; this might be the closure you need.*

I took my phone with shaky hands, which Alex probably noticed. Usually, I'm not self-conscious about whether my phone is with me or if it's lost, but this time, I suddenly felt unsafe. It wasn't until we were out of the café that I noticed it was already nighttime. It's 20:08 pm; we can finish this discussion in 10 minutes; I can go back to Alex, we leave, and call it a day.

"I saw the invitation that you sent me for your 21st birthday. I – I didn't want to reject it because I want us to stay on good terms and be friends like we have been managing for the past five years, but I don't want what happened seven years ago to happen again. I know I sound selfish, but I will have to reject this invitation. Don't get me wrong, I would love to attend..." That's weird. I know Nicholas is still talking, but I can't hear him anymore, and I'm starting to see everything blurred. He's laughing, but I can't hear him; he's moving his lips. I see it despite the blur that's getting worse, but I can't tell what he's saying. I tried to grab my phone and call Alex to come out and talk to me so that I could see if I could hear him, but my phone fell to the ground. I can't seem to be able to hold it. I look at Nicholas' face, and all I see is worry. He is coming near me. I still can't hear him, and before I realise it,

I cry in front of Nicholas again. At this point, I can't see anything, hear anything, or move. All I can feel is sadness and the warmth of my tears falling.

"Nicholas, I need Alex," I tried to scream, but apparently, there was no voice coming out of me. "Nicholas, Alex will know what's wrong with me," I tried again and again and again; nothing worked. Nicholas got close enough for me to be able to smell his signature citron fragrance. It feels like he is taking permission to touch me.

One tap. Two taps. Three. It's a code we created to ask for permission. We used this code back when I used to get panic attacks, which affected my hearing. Is that what's happening to me now? But they stopped for the past five years. They can't be back again; there is no trigger. But by the time I stopped thinking and tried making another effort to see my surroundings, Nicholas was already carrying me to what felt like the café.

Two taps, one tap, two taps. Alex's code is another code Alex and I created when I used to get panic attacks that required me to go to the hospital. But how are we going to the hospital if Nicholas put me on something which could be identified as a chair? Are they fighting? Am I causing them to fight? Is this all because of me?

I should have gotten over Nicholas and moved on. Having a 'first love' was wrong. It's all just an imagination I was believing in based on the romantic books I read. This entire situation is stupid. I should have listened to Alex and never sent the invitation to Nicholas. I'm so witless. I want to get up and apologise to Nicholas, but my body still won't, and my vision and hearing are still blurred. The ringing in my ears is getting worse, and I can feel the warmth of my tears again, which was gone when Alex tapped me.

"If you cared about Avène's mental health, you wouldn't take her out there *alone* and be so straightforward with stuff like that, knowing damn well she hasn't gotten over you yet." Just like that, I started hearing Alex's voice again. I need to stop them. This isn't right; this wasn't how the day was supposed to go. It's our friendship anniversary tomorrow; we aren't supposed to be spending it like this. This is all going wrong. I need to move, just for a second. I need to move. I just need my legs to work, although I'm starting to regain motion in other body parts. Come on. Come on.

I turn around as the blur starts to fade, and I see Alex moving towards Nicholas. Please, Alex. Please, Alex, don't. Alex, please. Come on. The minute I was able to move my legs again, I ran between the two of them. And suddenly, my mind went blank. My body went cold.

Chapter 2
Nicholas

"What happened to Avène? What did you say to her to affect her to the extent that her panic attacks are back?" Alex yelled as he saw me carrying Avène back in the café.

"I didn't do anything; we were just talking, and then it just happened," I growled as I placed her on the chair. Before I even finished doing so, Alex pushed me away from Avène. They say time changes people, but in the entire seven years, Alex's short temper never improved.

"Tell me what you talked about!" he yelled as he dragged me away from Avène. Alex and I were never able to be long-term friends who could stay together for more than a day. If he was short-tempered, I'm worse by double.

"We spoke about the invitation. I rejected it, but I did mention to her that it doesn't mean we can't be friends," I said as I felt my patience coming to an end. We are fighting and arguing about something that can't be changed while Avène needs help. If I knew

Alex would react like this and boss me around about what I said and didn't say without putting Avène's health first, then I would have taken her straight to the hospital.

"If you cared about Avène's mental health, you wouldn't take her out there *alone* and be so straightforward with stuff like that, knowing damn well she hasn't gotten over you yet," he said, looking confused about whether to get physical or not. I tried to control the situation, especially as we were in a café, but my patience and temper came to an end. Avène sat there in pain, not knowing what was going on, as we wasted our time arguing about who the bad guy was in this situation.

I closed the distance between the two of us and pinned him to the wall without realising I was choking him from the force generated by my hands. "Don't you ever decide whether I care about Avène's mental health or not? If you are jealous right now that there is a chance Avène and I might get together, then you are the one who doesn't care about Avène because she has a severe panic attack, and you are here arguing with me instead of looking for ways to get her to the hospital." My jaw tightened. Alex's feelings got hurt, and when he was hurt, he could do anything. I'm not scared, but I don't want any more trouble; we need to get Avène out of here and to the hospital.

As I turned around to get Avène from the chair I placed her on, she wasn't there. I turned around to look for her, and as I did, I saw that Alex was about to hammer me with the champagne bottle. I found him drinking when I just got in. But then there she is. Avène is between me and Alex, bleeding. For a moment, the entire café went silent, but the next, everyone crowded around her to see what's going on.

I snapped out of the shock and quickly bent down to carry Avène to the hospital. I look at Alex, who is on the floor drunk, regretful, and despairing while holding Avène close to him. The sight gives me this weird feeling in my heart that I haven't felt since that day.

"She needs you to be close to her, so stop regretting what has already happened, and let's take her to the hospital," I said as I carried Avène while Alex was walking beside me.

"Avène was asking about you while she had the panic attack. She also wanted to stop you from hurting me because she loves you." I drove the car while Alex held Avène in the backseat. Alex doesn't often cry, but tonight, he cried like he never did before.

"What do you mean?" Alex said, looking confused for many reasons.

"What I mean is, when I realised that Avène was having a panic attack, I focused on her lips to see if she was trying to say something because, just like in the past, she was unable to speak. While I focused, she was saying things like, 'Nicholas, I need Alex.' That's why I brought her to you in that state instead of immediately going to the hospital without letting you know. Before you get mad, I didn't want to tell you because I knew how you would react, but I didn't know this exact situation would be happening." I sighed as I took a U-turn. "Avène probably also knew how you would react, although she couldn't hear us. She knew that you and I were short-tempered to the point where one of us would get badly injured. That's why she forced herself to get up and take the hit for me, which you now feel guilty for. Believe me, even if I got hurt, you would react the same way but with a different type of guilt because although we fight a lot and in bad terms most of the time, I know that for both of us, deep down, we care about each other. I would protect you before you get hurt," I said as we parked in front of the hospital.

I turn around to Alex before I open the doors and say, "You're a mature adult now. Show us how much you have improved."

I open the door for Alex and help him get Avène out. I see an ER nurse pass by. I ran to her and explained the situation, so she helped us. We both run back to the car and get Avène in the wheelchair to take her to the ER unit. We registered her as a patient and let them figure out if she had a concussion or any injury and the reason why her panic attacks were back. Meanwhile, I calm Alex down and help him shower off Avène's blood that he's covered with.

"Hey Alex, wanna talk about it after you shower?" I said, after feeling that weird sensation in my heart again while seeing Alex walk away alone, covered in blood.

"Yeah, meet me at the cafeteria,"

"Thank you, and sorry for everything," Alex said while watching me pay for his coffee. He had argued with me for 10 minutes about who would pay for the other's coffee. I just stared at him.

"Why are you looking at me like that?" he said, looking confused. The innocence he had had since the first day I met him ten years ago felt like it was back, replacing the despair that he had when he was with Avène.

I smiled and said, "Welcome back, Alex Perovich." We got our coffees and sat together at a table quietly. After some minutes of complete silence, I decided to address the elephant in the room.

"So, for Avène, you can see her. I'm not purposefully bringing you here to take you away from her. It's just that she needs to run some tests, and when doctors tell us what's going on with her, we will go. But while they do that, you and I need to discuss what has been going on for seven years," I nervously said while fidgeting with my tissue.

Although I usually don't get nervous during conversations like these, for some reason, when I'm talking to Alex or Avène, I forget what to say or how to act, which is unusual.

"These past 4 hours have been full of events, making me realise that I need to stop being so overprotective towards Avène. I know we have been so close forever; she is like a sister to me. But I realised that we are adults now, and Avène needs to get a feel of how adult life truly works. I'm sorry, Nicholie. I know that because I care so much about Avène, our friendship was affected. I didn't mean to hurt you; I wasn't in my right mind," he stated with a shaky voice. His apology gave me that weird feeling again while realising that I've been longing for this side of Alex, where he isn't self-centred. His statement is right; they both need to drift slightly apart as they will both have real jobs next year. Moving forward in life is hard and appalling to everyone, which I understand, but Alex must move forward and develop a strong masculine personality while taking care of Avène.

It may seem to many people that their loved one will stay with them for a lifetime, but the reality is everything comes to an end; the drip always stops.

Chapter 3
Avène

"Avène Valikova?" she yelled with her southern accent. My art teacher always had this weird accent, partially because she is from Texas, but also because she wants to become Mandy from 'Young Sheldon.'

"Yes, I'm here!" I yelled to make sure I registered. I've been absent for over a month with a sick leave because of my asthma condition getting worse and my brother Denis Valikova getting admitted to a mental hospital due to his autism and bipolar disorders worsening. This is the first time his condition has worsened to the point he needs to be admitted. I feel very confused right now with all that's happening, but I know one thing for sure. Denis will be staying at the hospital for a while. I could have used more time to get my thoughts sorted and make sure I'm well enough to go back to school and socialise, but I've been falling behind with schoolwork, and I've started feeling this strange feeling where my throat tightens, and my chest aches. I've also started to lose motivation to do things, so I decided to come to school and speak to the counsellor and my favourite teacher, Ms Savanna and Mr Michael.

Mr Michael is a fun guy to be around. He reads books I read and even watches the movie I liked and told him about! Our favourite one to talk about is Argylle.

"Ms, can I go to Mr Michael for a couple of minutes to discuss something urgent? I promise to catch up on all the work, you know me. I love art." I walked to her desk and smiled.

"Don't take too long," she said while signing documents.

I ran to the door without telling Anastasia where I was going.

I walked in the silent hall towards Mr Michael's office, and I felt empty. I didn't know if I wanted to cry because I was overwhelmed, if I wanted to leave school, or if I wanted someone to tell me everything will be okay. But I reached his office and knocked.

"Yessir, come in, come in," he cheered. "Oh, Avène! Is it a thumbs up or down for today?" I motioned thumbs down.

Mr Michael and I have this thing of thumbs up and down where I would motion to him how I feel about things. It's been a year since we started doing this because, although I am social and have no problems making friends and being close with teachers, I still find it hard to communicate my emotions.

"Want to talk about it? Is that why you're here and why you have been absent for an entire month?" he asked so quickly I almost didn't understand the last phrase.

"Yeah, my brother had a very bad tantrum on January 25th, worse than the ones he usually gets. I was so terrified, but I couldn't show it because both my parents were already in a chaotic moral..." I spoke and spoke until I had no words left. I felt so exhausted that I just wanted to take a break from life, like being in a coma for at least three days.

"I think you are falling into the depression path, which is why you are starting to lose interest in things. Depression leads to chest tightness and all those symptoms as it gets accompanied by panic attacks. Avène, you are so exhausted, and you must realise that. Ms. Savanna and I are here to help you. The sooner you admit to yourself that you are sick and need help, the sooner you will be making progress in your recovery journey..." Mr. Michael never sounded so serious before; he is giving me a mental health session. He must think *I am* severely sick, and I don't want to hear his lecture any longer.

"Yes, understood. I'll reach out to Ms. Savanna; I know I am sick. Thank you for your time," I rushed.

"Avène," I stopped, heading to the door. "What's really going on?" he said, sounding completely sincere and scared to hurt me more.

"Everything is wrong. My entire life is wrong. This tantrum was the last straw. Everything in my life is horrible. My mother treats me awfully all the time, and only when she feels like it she would then treat me the way a mother should. My brother is ill; my friends aren't really my friends. My dad is the only person who is acting the way he is supposed to. The same goes for my teachers, but outside of school, all my teachers are useless. I feel like a robotic monster because although all this is going on, I still do well academically as an artist, musician, and athlete. It scares me. I know I should be grateful, but it scares me." I sobbed while feeling the symptoms coming back.

The chest tightness got so bad this time that I fell.

"Avène, I can't believe you forgot about me. You only message me when your friends don't include you in their plans or when something is going on," Alex mumbled.

I wanted to answer him, but I couldn't. It looks as if he is going somewhere far away, and I can't move. I feel like a ghost. Alex, please don't leave me alone again. Please. I will do anything to fix this. I'm sorry for everything, but he went further till he disappeared.

I can't see anything now; I'm alone somewhere dark where I can't move, speak, or feel anything. Am I dying? Is this it? Is this how my life ends?

"Ms Avène?" someone whispered. "Can you hear me?" someone far away mumbled.

"Open your eyes if you can hear me," another mumble.

"Ms Avène, open your eyes." The voice became clear.

"You must open your eyes now," the voice demanded.

I gradually opened them.

Chapter 4
Nicholas

"Is this Ms. Avène Valikova's guardian?" the nurse asked on the phone.

"Yes, it is," I replied, sounding hopeful.

"I've called to inform you that Ms Avène woke up and is asking for you and someone called Alex Perovich. If you can, please do come and check on her," she averred.

"Yes, we'll be coming. What room is it?"

"221"

"Nicholas, Alex," Avène said, sounding exhausted.

"How do you feel now?" Alex asked while looking away. Avène's doctors told us that she has a concussion due to the champagne bottle shattering on her head with strong force, which makes Alex want to avoid eye contact as he feels ashamed.

"I'm okay. Did the doctors tell you guys *something*?" she emphasised the word 'something' as if we aren't supposed to know what it is.

Alex and I looked at each other, and we decided I should talk to her since this whole situation started when we spoke.

"Yeah, we know something. Exactly what they told you. Your panic attacks are back because of what I said to you, and your concussion is due to you coming between me and Alex. They also told us you were stuck in a flashback for over an hour. We sat in the cafeteria, thinking we hadn't gotten any call yet just because they were running more tests. What we don't know is what the flashback was and what part specifically triggered your panic attack," I summarised.

"I'm so sorry for everything I put you two through. I didn't mean to, but my mental health just gave up on me, as you can see. Nicholas, it's not that I didn't like what you said to me. I was scared because it felt like what happened seven years ago was reoccurring. For you, Alex, we need to fix your temper; otherwise, I'm not mad at either of you." She laughed.

This is one of the things that attracts me to Avène. No matter what situation she's in, she always smiles and makes other people smile, brightening everywhere she goes.

"So, do we all feel ready to solve whatever has been going on?" Alex asked, looking at me and Avène.

"No, not now," Avène blurted.

"Not my thing," I commented right after her.

"Okay, and Nicholas, please bring down your ego, booger."

"*Booger*? I thought you had got over saying that word. The last time you said it was when you were 17," I drawled.

"Shut up, you know I hate swearing, so I used 'booger' to swear at you," he sounded embarrassed.

"Yeah, sure. And my ego isn't higher than it's supposed to be. I just simply hate problem-solving conversations. They aren't my thing," Alex growled, acting like he was fervid at my statement. Avène and I look at him and laugh. We haven't had a moment like this in a while. I wish this could last slightly longer, but I must snap out of this imagination and return to my reality. If my father, Anderson Patrick, finds out about this, he could destroy my entire career position.

My father, Anderson Patrick, is the founder of the PATRICKUS jewellery company, and I earned the CEO position one year ago after multiple votes. PATRICKUS was founded in 1960, so we are old-money billionaires. After this company was formed in 2000, my father built a club that was only for people with supreme titles, which is called Elysium. Elysium is different from other clubs in the world in every way, and it's the best in L.A; the exterior and interior are made from diamonds twenty-four karat gold, and the door handles are designed from pure pearls.

Every decoration in Elysium costs millions and can only be found there, but all this comes with a price at the end.

My father knows Avène as she works there as a bartender to cover her university costs, but he also knew her before since she used to be my friend in grade 8. My family was fine with it, but if they found out this time, they wouldn't be, since she is considered *poor*, which could harm our reputation.

"I must leave now. It was nice seeing you two again. Get better soon, Avène, and I'm sorry. Happy early 21st birthday." I handed her the flowers I bought for her earlier, along with a letter.

"Thank you," she replied, sounding breathless.

"Take care, Nicholie, and I'm sorry for today," Alex murmured.

"Yeah, thanks, man, and please don't murmur next time. Say it clearly," I suggested.

I walked out without looking in Avène's direction. I feel horrible for leaving her alone while she is hospitalised, but I'd feel worse if father finds out what I've been up to.

I checked my phone as I headed towards the parking lot and found out that I had twenty-five missed calls from Anderson, ten from my secretary, and five from my fiancée. Unbelievable. I didn't realise that it's been

7 hours since I left home. I start by calling Anderson since his temper is shorter than my fiancée's.

"Good evening, father," I hesitantly spoke when he picked up the phone.

"Good evening, son. Care to tell me where you've been?" he demanded. "Yes, father. I had to go to Rodeo Drive to buy Sophia the Bulgari Diamond Swan Necklace as our engagement present," I falsified. "Well done. You should take care of your fiancée and make sure she will stay beside you. One custom-made diamond ring won't impress a girl," he cheered.

"Yes, father. I'll be home soon. Tell Sophia not to worry," I said while assuming he is home with Sophia and hung up the phone before hearing his 'farewell.'

Sophia is the girl Anderson chose for me to get engaged to. Naturally, I was forced to do so because no one in Patrick's family was allowed to stay single at the age of twenty-three. If I asked to marry Avène, I would lose my title and my entire life, so I had to go with what Anderson chose. Sophia is a good person, but she thinks our relationship is built on true love despite it being an arranged marriage. We act like we sleep on the same bed, but once I'm sure Sophia is fast asleep, I go and sleep on the couch beside the bed Sophia is sleeping on. Before she wakes up at around 10 am, I go next to her at 9:30 so she doesn't notice anything.

Heretofore, I've been hiding my literal feelings quite well for over seven months, as Avène and I haven't spoken for that long. But when she sent me her birthday invitation via email two weeks ago, the silence was broken. Especially after today, I expect things to get worse. Sophia and I have two months left till we get married, and once that happens, I know for sure I will never get to talk to Avène anymore.

"Mr Nicholas, you're back. I'll let your father know," the security guard at the front gate implied.

"Yes, thank you. Tell him I'll change and head straight to the office," I handed him the car keys and walked towards the mansion's front door.

I opened the door and immediately went to the left staircase that led to my suite. I can hear music coming from the suite, which means Sophia is in there. As I was about to reach the room, I heard the music clearly, and it reminded me of Avène. The song is "Comptine d'un autre été" (nursery rhyme from another summer). I used to do a duet with Avène for this song; I would play the piano and, for her, the violin.

I open the door and walk in while hiding the Swan Necklace that I managed to get within 5 minutes. "Sophia, look who's back," I drawled. She stopped doing her nails, paused the music, and looked my way, already smiling. "Welcome back, Nichol! You had me worried sick," she was expecting me to go to her and give her our usual greeting kiss, but with all that's been happening with Avène and Alex, it was too excruciating for me to act like I love Sophia more than anyone.

"I have something for you that you'll like," I whispered to her while bringing out the gift bag. She comes to me, takes the bag from my hand, and opens it. "No way. *THE BULGARI SWAN NECKLACE? ARE YOU SERIOUS?*" she yelled with her cute, squeaky voice while jumping around, forgetting the rule in the house '*to always act elegant, even if the head of the house isn't around.*'

"Nichol, this is so sweet; I'm speechless. This is the most iconic gift I've ever received. Does this mean I'm the only person in this world who owns this?" she asks as if that's the important thing, more than the gift. Although Sophia is a good fiancée who has never caused any sort of trouble, she is the type of girl who only cares about showing what they have and what they don't, unlike Avène.

Avène didn't come from a rich family, but her family had enough funds to allow them to purchase and have a luxurious life. However, at the age of 16, when Avène and I started talking again, she felt like she was burdening her family, so she decided to get a part-time job, which was writing books and trying to publish them while also giving music lessons to children. She earned enough to cover the costs of her brother Denis and her university studies, so her father ended up paying only for housing and social life. But this year, which is Avène's last year of university before she becomes an official sports journalist, she has earned a scholarship while working at Elysium, so it's allowing her to gain a lot more money. Yet she was never a showboat.

As I came back to my senses and stopped comparing Sophia to Avène, I found Sophia upset next to the speaker, changing her song to *Can't Help Falling in Love* Classic. She increased the volume, put her bag down, and came towards me, asking for permission to dance with her a waltz. We've always done this whenever she felt unsettled; we would never talk about the feelings bothering us. We would either perform a waltz, or I would go to my office until we both calmed down. But this time was different; Sophia wasn't calming down.

Chapter 5
Avène

Just like that, Nicholas was gone, and the room went quiet. I looked down at the beautiful bouquet that had a mix of tulips, daisies, and daffodils. While I took the letter out of the bouquet, I realised all these flowers have a common meaning: forgiveness and a new beginning. Nicholas always buys flowers with meanings that resemble the event taking place, and whenever we spend time together, we would talk about the meanings of flowers. But never have I ever thought that Nicholas would give me a forgiveness bouquet.

"*Dear Avene,*

I don't know how you would react to what I'm going to say in this letter, as you will probably read it by the time I'm gone, but I hope it doesn't worsen your condition.

I'm sorry for everything that has happened since the first day we met. I know I always just keep on apologising, but each time I do, I mean it. It's just that things keep on happening, which makes me look like a bad person and prevents me from getting to know more of you.

Most importantly, I'm sorry for today. I didn't mean to be harsh or hurt you like that, but I just can't come to your birthday or meet with you and Alex tomorrow to celebrate our friendship anniversary; yes, I didn't forget. And in two months, I don't think I can ever see you again.

Anyways, you've always been an amazing person to me and everyone around you. You always brighten up my world like sunshine. Keep on shining, Avene. Don't let your health, me, or anyone make you stop shining. Shine like the star you are born to be.

Take care,
Nicholas"

"Hey Alex, how do you get over your first love?" I got up from bed and slowly walked towards the waste bin. Alex kept staring at me for a minute, confused as to why I got up while holding the bouquet and letter, although I still felt unwell. I looked down at what I was holding and back at him. "I'm not going anywhere; I just want to throw these away."

"Are you okay? What did he write down on that letter?" he sounded worried and confused, especially since we all had a fun moment before Nicholas left. I didn't want to worry Alex, but I still walked to the bin and repeated my question. "How do you get over your first love?"

"I don't know, Avène. I haven't had my first love yet, and you know that." Although Alex tried to hide it as much as possible, he sounded like he was about to cry. Alex has always been emotional and has a short temper, but never as extreme as today. I know that he feels sorry and guilty for what he did to me, but that shouldn't make him despair to this extent. I know he can't control it, but it hurts me because I can't imagine how he would react if he found out the truth about what the doctors really diagnosed me with.

CHAPTER 6
Avène

It's been five days since I was diagnosed with Glioblastoma with a time limit of 3 months. It's also been five days since I was admitted to this hospital for a completely different reason. Today, however, I get to return to my normal life. The only difference is that I want to pursue everything I've ever dreamed of while keeping my diagnosis a secret before my time runs out.

For most people, their life gets morbid once they know they've been diagnosed with a deadly disease that has no cure, but I'm part of the 5% that continues to live the usual way even when they know they are dying. I mean, it's human nature, and I can't stop it from happening or change my fate. It's unfair that I can't figure skate anymore in 3 months' time, or experience how it feels to be a professional sports journalist since I won't graduate from university until next year, or get to have children I've dreamed of having for ages, neither get to say goodbye to my parents since they live in Paris while I live in Boston, or experience my 21st birthday I've been planning for. But I'm not the first to die at the age of 20; some other people have died way younger and had a more unfair life than me. This is the thought that is supporting me in not breaking down and being able to do this alone.

I've been craving Wingstop with some Crumbl cookies as a dessert, so I decided to call Anastasia, Charlotte, Isabella, Evelyn, Cora, and Eleanor to go with me and have our little gossip session. In high school, we used to have these gossip sessions every week on Fridays or rarely on Saturdays if we forced Eleanor to get out of her tutor sessions.

"Brings back memories, guys!" Eleanor cheered, or more like making us deaf with her volume. "Yeah, it does. Reminds me of that one time you stole my last piece of Hawaiian-flavoured wing, knowing damn well I can't eat spice," Evelyn stated with the most unvaried tone.

Eleanor Gomez is our very "busy" Hispanic friend who talks all day long about how she wants to build her own makeup business and become Kylie Jenner 2.0. She's a chatterbox who uses English and Spanish to communicate with us, although we don't understand Spanish except for swear words. As for Evelyn Martin, I think she'll become a gamer soon. I tried playing Fortnite with her on my old, tarnished Nintendo Switch, and she's unbelievably good. To be honest, it makes sense; she even goes to a gaming university. I know it's crazy. Eleanor and Evelyn are both twenty and born on September 29th, which is probably why, although they have different humour, they still share the same brain full of insanity.

"Insane," Anastasia and I said at the same time. Anastasia is my best, best, best, *best* friend. She's been with me since grade 10, and now we are both doing our master's degree at the same time and at the same university. She wants to be a sports psychologist. She's 23 years old yet acts like a 7-year-old who never ages.

"How do you remember something that happened four years ago? I don't even remember what I ate *yesterday*," I asked, genuinely concerned about her memory. "I remember it because she's the only and first person to ever steal my last wing. And I don't have a fish memory like you. Well, I do, but only at specific times." As always, talking like a teenager, although Evelyn is 20, she'll forever be her 14-year-old self.

"UGH! *Best* wings everrrr!" Evelyn moaned loudly, embarrassing Cora and Charlotte, who were sat next to her. "Evelyn, I swear to God, next time you moan at this place, I'll shove the wing up your ass," Cora said, sounding serious. Charlotte looked at both with a grin, gradually lightening her facial expressions. "Yeah, Eve, I dare you to!" She exhilarated Evelyn but startled all of us.

Charlotte Schneider is a marine lover and wanna-be marine biologist. She's 21 years old but acts 30 most of the time, and there are times like now when she acts like a 10-year-old. Her father owns a boat, so he takes her every weekend to sail, swim, do Scuba diving, or talk to the marine animals. Whoever sees Charlotte knows that she likes the marine; her freckles and body build voice her obsession. Cora Mills is similar; she used to be a wanna-be marine biologist because she wanted to meet an orca but decided to go for ecology. Her body build and personality are so soft, which helps her voice the message she wants people to understand she's the future Jane Goodall or Greta Thunberg 2.0.

"Shocker," Isabella gasped. Isabella Wang is another wanna-be psychologist. This girl changed career choices five times in high school and ten times in university. She went from wanting to be a criminologist to a journalist, then to a neurologist, and finally to a psychologist, and the list never ends. Hopefully, psychology is what she truly wants this time; otherwise, soon, I won't be able to give her any more advice sessions. But at least she's the youngest, currently 19 years old.

"So, Avène, wanna tell us about Nicholai?" Evelyn drawled inquisitively.

I looked around and sighed. "Nothing much happened, guys. He came to the café, rejected the invite, and left, but I felt lightheaded, so Alex took me to the hospital." I kept on paltering for an hour until we left to get some Crumbl cookies and call it a night.

Thank God we ended the night with no one stealing one of Evelyn's Hawaiian-flavoured wings.

CHAPTER 7
Nicholas

"Apologies? You want to go where?" I was absolutely startled by Sophia's call. I received her call in the middle of a meeting, which is unusual. I excused myself to go to the bathroom to answer, but I never thought it would be just her asking me a moronic question.

"Bali. Can we go there for at least three days? Prithee." I sighed while looking at myself in the bathroom's mirror, realising that my eye bags were worsening as the days passed by. "Are you serious? You interrupted my meeting just to ask me a question that could've waited till I got home. I thought you were smarter than this." I hung up the phone without allowing her to waste more of my time, fixed my tie, and returned to my meeting.

I've been drowning myself in tasks for the past three weeks to avoid someone from occupying my thoughts, but it hasn't been working. Nothing works, and no work crisis, meeting, or workload keeps me from thinking about that person. I've been wondering if she's okay with taking care of the flowers I gave her or if she's also thinking about me right now. Her birthday is tomorrow, and I do have the urge to go apologise to her and just have a fresh start, but my logistics are holding me back; the guilt is taking over me. I haven't seen Sophia or Anderson for the past week because of my workload, so I haven't gone to get some fresh air, proper sleep, or do my usual fitness or proper nutrition, just salad deliveries.

So far, no one has asked me if there is something going on or if I've ever gone home in the past week, but I'm sure that they have noticed since the third day I haven't left this office, judging by the pitying eyes they look at me with. Today, after my call with Sophia, I returned to my meeting with the CEO of Valhalla Company to sign a deal. Throughout the entire duration of the meeting, he looked at me with pity. I almost restricted him from seeing me again, didn't agree to sign the deal, nor did I keep him alive.

My phone's vibration got me out of my thoughts temporarily; I check it and see that it's Anderson.

Anderson: *Take Sophia to Bali. It'll be like a honeymoon, especially since your wedding is in 2 months.*

Nicholas: *Will do. I'll take her by Thursday and reschedule all my meetings.*

Anderson: *Proud of you. Hope to see you soon at home.*

Nicholas: *I'll come tomorrow.*

Anderson: *Farewell.*

Seeing Anderson take time from his leisure to text me made me confident that, although I'm going to hate this trip, I must accept because Sophia would get accepted as well as Anderson, which will create more problem-solving situations for me, which I hate. Four days left till Thursday, and at last I'm going to get occupied with all the meetings that are going to be preponed.

"Good evening, Cassie. I have an urgent trip to Bali on Thursday, which will take three days, so please postpone all my meetings until the next four days," I firmly requested.

"Yes, sir. Consider it done by tomorrow," she accepted immediately, which now confirms that the next 4 days are going to be occupied with work thoughts and not Avène.

CHAPTER 8
Avène

"Bali is currently the most visited Island, exceeding the number of people visiting the Maldives..." Bali. Bali is a place I've wanted to visit for ages, but my parents never agreed, and I find myself spending so much on useless things that I don't have enough money left to go on a trip. But this time, the news reporter made me want to make sure I tick it off the bucket list I've created of all the things I want to do within these three months.

Bucket list:

- *Visit Bali*
- *Eat Tteokbokki*
- *Publish my book*
- *Compete in gymnastics*
- *Become a sports journalist*
- *Spend fun time with Alex*

- *Gossip more with the girls*
- *Never see Nicholas again*

I kept staring at the bucket list as I thought of what else to add until I got the perfect idea of how to get to Bali. "Hey, Alex. You know how you told me you would allow me to choose my birthday gift this year, no matter how expensive it is?"

"Yes?" he answered, concerned.

"Let's go to Bali!" I cheered excitedly. I waited for his reply, which felt like it took ages, but it was only a couple of seconds until I heard him sighing a yes!

"So, when do you want to go?" he asked, as if he was free on all days, just like how he used to act when we were in high school. Alex would have important events and things coming up, but no matter what, he would always put me first. I don't know if it was the pity of not having a normal family environment or if it was just genuine love, but I hated it when he acted this way.

"Be honest, on what day are you free? And for how long?" I asked with a serious tone to show him that nothing is wrong with being busy and letting the other person wait.

"Upcoming Thursday. We can stay for three days only, but we can stay longer if you would like to." He rushed his reply so fast I almost didn't understand what he said. I took a deep breath and answered him to end the call. "Okay then, book a flight on Thursday anytime you want, and we'll stay there for three days. Thanks, Alex, means a lot."

"Anytime. Take care," the call ended there, and I got up to go get some fresh air. I suddenly felt emotional.

"One Spanish latte and white chocolate chunk cookie, please." I decided to walk to Ben's cookies, which is ten blocks away from my apartment, to get my favourite order while I sit there and try to finish writing my book. I need around 100 pages before I can start editing it and achieve my goal. I've been lacking inspiration, so this coffee and cookie should give me something.

It's been 2 hours since I opened my laptop to write something, and to my surprise, I've achieved writing ten pages! I've finished drinking my coffee and savouring my cookie, so I check my phone to see what time it is to plan what to do next since my mood has enlightened. It's 17:23 on a Sunday; I feel like shopping, so I call Anastasia to see if she's free.

"Yes? What's up?" Anastasia picked up the phone after three rings.

"Wanna hang out in 30 minutes at the seaport?" I begged so that she wouldn't give me an excuse just because she was too lazy to dress up. "I'm busy. I'm going on a blind date in an hour, sorry." I hung up to carry on my mission to get someone from the group to go to the seaport with me. I call Isabella next since she's *always* free.

As expected, before the first ring even finished, she picked up. "Wanna hang out at the seaport with me, Isa?" I didn't get a chance to catch a breath before I heard her reply, typical Isabella. "Of course! I'd never say no. What time?"

"Meet me in 30 minutes." Boston Seaport is my favourite place to spend time during winter because of the Christmas decorations, but during summer, such as now, it's my favourite because of the sales and memories made.

I got up to walk home and drop off my laptop before getting a cab to head to the seaport, but as I pushed my chair back, I unexpectedly felt a sudden headache followed by nausea.

This can't be happening, my inner voice yelled. The doctors did warn me about my symptoms worsening each day I live without getting admitted to the hospital or taking any medication to slow it down, but I didn't think it would happen this soon.

I pushed myself to go to the bathroom to hide there until the pain alleviated, but it kept on getting worse until I started vomiting to the extent I felt like passing out. However, after what I think was about 10 minutes, I stopped vomiting but couldn't get up due to my body feeling heavy, as if I'd done a 4-hour workout. I allowed myself to sit there and cry for a while longer. I felt like the 14-year-old me again, where I suffered with severe panic attacks, except that this time, I'm sure I'll die soon.

Another 5 minutes passed before I gradually walked back to my seat to pack away my laptop and run home to meet Isa. I thought I had only wasted 15 minutes in the bathroom, but after I checked my phone, I realised those symptoms had lasted for 40 minutes, with ten missed calls and 50+ messages from Isa.

Isabella: *girl, are you okay? You're never late. What happened to Russian time management?*

Avène: *Sorry, but Russians also have life consequences, so I'm allowed to be late occasionally, Isa.*

Isabella: *Fine, just hurry up. I'll be waiting at Nero!*

Avène: *whatever suits you, don't order for me!!*

Isabella: *Nice humour.*☹

I reached home, grabbed my purse, and ordered an Uber. Isabella will murder me today; I've never been late to any hangouts before, so her Q&A today will be a long one.

"Nice time management, Ms Valikova," Isabella checked her watch and looked up at me again with an inch-by-inch smirk that started to cover her face. "35 minutes late; you need to owe me something, Valikova. This is unacceptable," she commanded, like how a king commands his soldiers.

"So, I'm a soldier now? Your Highness, please have mercy on me." We laughed as I pushed her up so that we could do some shopping before her questionnaire started the next time we sat. Isabella may be the youngest of us, but she is the first to get the feeling that something is wrong. I like that about her, but right now, I'm dreading it.

We spoke while searching for the shop we specifically wanted to see today, and after around 5 minutes of walking, we reached it. Le Labo, I love their perfumes, shampoos, conditioners, and *oh. My. God,* their candles! Literal perfection. My goal for today is to walk out of their shop with Santal 33 and 26; they are expensive, but I desperately want to use them before it's time.

CHAPTER 9
Nicholas

One day left until Bali. For the past three days, they have been insanely hectic, but today, I have nothing left to do. So, Avène is back, living rent-free in my thoughts, but I won't allow it.

"Hello Cassie, I'm going to step out for the rest of the day, so whoever visits the office, tell them I'm busy with an urgent matter." I've done equestrianism ever since I was three years old, as every member of Patrick's family must choose a sport between the ages 2 and 3; otherwise, the head of the family will choose the sport for you, and you would have to stick to it for a lifetime. Thankfully, I was born the most talented and successful child, so even at a young age, I knew that equestrianism had my heart. I don't do it professionally anymore, as I've achieved enough through it in the past 15 years, but whenever I need to keep myself busy or sort out my thoughts, that's the place I go to and spend hours riding on my horse named "Raven."

"Yes, sir. I won't tell them that you went horse riding," she teased. Cassie has been my secretary for the past four years, but before that, she was Anderson's for ten years. That's why I let her get away with her jokes; otherwise, she would've been fired a long time ago.

I drove to the manège and went immediately to Raven. "It's been a while, Raven. Let's get you ready to get out of this barn," I kept on talking to Raven while preparing her to go with me to the forest.

I look into her eyes one final time before I mount her. "Alright, buddy, let's do this," I excitedly said. I may be dry or not very humorous to others, but with Raven, my childish personality will forever be shown in front of her.

We've now reached the forest, so I finally open up to Raven, as I know no one will overhear the conversation. "Raven, this might shock you, but Avène and I met, spoke *and* had a whole situation going on." Raven replies with a neigh, which translates to "*SHOCKER*," or at least that's what I interpreted it as.

"Yeah, I know Raven. But you know what's more of a shocker? Because I'm afraid of Anderson and Sophia taking away everything from me that I've worked so hard for, I wrote a letter to Avène, which I'm sure hurt her a lot. I feel horrible for doing that and for showing this weakness. Feels like I'm not even acting like how a man is supposed to." Raven neighs again, but this time it's a long one, which I interpreted as, "What do you mean? Are you saying you want to tell them that you're gay?"

"No, Raven. I'm not gay; I'm just saying I'm not acting as tough as a man is supposed to be. But in this scenario, I think it would've turned out better if only I was gay. I wouldn't be forced to marry Sophia nor have feelings for Avène that I'm not allowed to show," I sighed and waited patiently to hear Raven's reply. After a second, she replied with a longer neigh, translating to, "You are a man; people are meant to be different. That's what makes us human. If you and Avène are truly meant for each other, the universe will pull you two together, even if it's going to happen in another life. Just never doubt yourself." I smiled for the first time in a while after realising how unstable I would look to someone if they were to pass by and hear my conversation.

"Anyways, I'm travelling to Bali tomorrow and will stay there for three days with Sophia because Anderson insisted, so I won't be spending much time with you until sometime next week. You know, work pressure too when I come back," I enunciated while caressing her. She neighed right after I finished talking; this time, the neigh had no translation, just a sigh. "Let's get you back to the barn; I have to get going."

We arrived at the barn, and I decided to clean Raven before I left. Cleaning her is somehow therapeutic; it leaves me with some of my sanity.

Once I was done cleaning her, I bid my farewell and headed home to show our maid what I wanted to be packed in my suitcase and to send some final emails.

I reach home and hear Sophia singing from our suite, clarifying that she is euphoric for tomorrow. As I head towards the stairs to go to Sophia, I see Anderson sitting in the living room, greeting me with a smile.

"Good evening, father," I formally spoke as I stopped heading to the stairs and went towards the living room instead.

"Good evening, son. Ready for your trip tomorrow?" he gestured for me to sit next to him. Anderson and I barely have moments like these – no reason – I just simply hate them.

"Yes, father. I was about to go pack my suitcase,"

"Then, apologies for holding you back. Go ahead and check on Sophia as well," he gestured towards the stairs. "Farewell, enjoy your trip and refresh," Anderson said, tapping on my shoulder. "Forget about work, too; your eyebags are worsening. Don't think I haven't noticed."

"Thank you. I'll try my best to enjoy and relax. Take care," I forced a smile and excused myself to head to my suite.

Anderson and I don't have a father-and-son relationship like others. Ever since my mother died when I was five years old, Anderson became strict. I always thought maybe it was just trauma, and he doesn't want to lose his son as well – well, that's what I thought until last year – when I found out he was the reason my mother died. He murdered her over funds.

My mother had a heart of gold. She was one of the "perfect mums," answered all my needs, was kind, and most importantly, she gave me the affection I needed. Without her teaching me all the necessities at such a young age, I wouldn't be the CEO of our company today. She would always remind me of this metaphor, "You just have to consider the world a stage and act accordingly." To this day, I go by it.

Anderson doesn't know I know the truth of my mother's death, as I've been acting neutral, and that's the plan until I find the perfect moment to get back revenge. Anderson will forever be one of my most hated people in this world; he's the villain in my act.

I opened my suite's door, and there she was, singing, not knowing what family she got herself into. However, Sophia is a showboat, so if she has what satisfies her, I don't think she would mind sleeping next to a murderer holding a gun.

"Sophia, I'm home," I declared as I went to the walk-in closet to change my clothes and start packing.

I think I won't call a maid to help me pack after all. "Did you pack yet? What are you doing?" I screamed over the loud music, so she finally heard me.

"Welcome back, Nichol! Yes, I packed everything since yesterday, and today I packed my camera. So now that I'm done, I decided to blast some music while I redo my nails and match their aesthetics to Bali." She lowered the speaker's volume so that I could hear what she was saying. "You need to start packing right now, though. It's already late. What are you doing?"

"I'm packing. I'll come over to you when I'm done."

I walked over to Sophia once I finished packing and checked how her nail session was going before I headed downstairs to grab something to eat. I spent the entire day with Raven, so I forgot to eat, as usual.

"Let me see your progress," I cheerily said, bending down to see how far she had got with her nails so that I could calculate how much more time she needed to finish them.

It's already 1 am, and I'm exhausted, so I can't wait for Sophia to fall asleep. "Looks like Bali vibes! Come on, you should finish up soon; you need some sleep before our 8 am flight," I caressed her hair gently. "I'll head downstairs to grab a snack and be back."

"I'll make these nails look cutely elegant, and by the time you come back, you will find me fast asleep; I promise," she said with sincerity, which made me feel guilty for a moment.

CHAPTER 10
Avène

I can't believe this... me... in Bali – shut up, that sounds like a dream. Three hours left till I breathe Bali's air.

"Alex."

"Yes," he drawled. "What is it this time?" I've been annoying him with questions for the past 19 hours, so it's fair for him to feel fed up. I don't blame him.

"Slap me," I commanded while showing him which part of my cheek I wanted him to slap. "Slap me and tell me this is real."

"You're mentally unstable, Avène," he said. He turned around and faced me. I thought he would slap me, but instead, he just pinched me. "It's real, Ms. delusional," he drawled, turning back to face his screen.

I've always wanted to visit Bali, but what kept me away wasn't financial; it was my family. My family always loved travelling and exploring the world. They travelled the entire of Africa and half of Europe. It was fun, but sometimes it got overboard. I begged them to go to Bali and England at various times, but each time, the answer would be either, "Next year, Avène, we promise," or "Your brother won't be able to handle the time zone there."

My brother was always put first before me. I was always seen as the '*daughter that should be able to handle everything.*' When I started getting panic attacks, they weren't very worried; they just signed me up for therapy. But as that developed into self-harm, my father was the most worried, doing his role as a father trying to help.

Once my mental health stopped affecting my everyday life, or more like once I controlled my mental health and stopped being affected in front of them, everything went back to how it usually was. Mother started putting all the blame on me, father was still supportive but not in all necessities, and my brother's health had only kept on worsening, so the entire focus stayed on him for about six years.

My relationship with my family is still in a rocky zone, but lately, I've been wondering how they'd react if they found out I'm dying in three months. Would they be sad, concerned, regretful, or will they not care at all? But anyway, that's just curiosity. Right now, I'm thrilled to spend the next three days with Alex in Bali. Still feels like a dream.

"Avène, we're here," Alex said, pulling me out of my thoughts.

"What do you mean, we're here?"

"We arrived."

"Arrived where?" I asked, confused about what I was doing on an aeroplane with Alex alone. When did I even get here? "Why are we on an aeroplane?"

Alex sits back down next to me with concern in his eyes. "We're in Bali. Avène, are you joking?"

I stare at him while carefully thinking what to say next – wait...is this another symptom? Forgetfulness? Seriously? A symptom when I'm finally at the place I've been dying to visit. Over my dead body, will I allow something or someone to ruin this trip? "Of course, I'm joking. I just wanted to see your reaction," I laughed, tensing over Alex's frown.

"Don't do that again. Now, come on, let's go breathe some Bali air!" He breathed and handed me my backpack.

My memory is still not back, but so far, acting like 'neutral' Avène is going okay. We got our suitcases and headed to the hotel.

"Alex, for how many days are we staying here?" I genuinely asked, thinking that I originally didn't know.

"You've got to be joking. Are you serious? Aren't you the one who asked when I am busy again, and so we decided to stay here for three days?" he angrily said.

Oh, shit. I really can't keep on having these symptoms.

"Jesus, I'm just kidding. Calm down," I neutrally said.

CHAPTER 11
Avène

We arrived at the hotel, and I was finally regaining my memory. So, when the receptionist asked for my ID, I remembered which pocket I had placed it in. I left Alex to continue checking in as I rushed to the bathroom to drink my medicine before another symptom took place.

I feel horrible for scaring Alex twice and for keeping the truth hidden from him, but it's all for the best. I can die in peace while no one is hurt. I'm starting to feel regret for making him bring me to Bali when something wrong could have happened at any time, but I refuse for that to be a reality. Alex and I will enjoy these three days in Bali, and we will leave here happier.

I drank my medicine, and once I calmed down and sorted out my thoughts, I went back to the reception to find Alex. After a few steps, I found Alex sitting by a piano placed near the entry; it reminded me of him, Nicholas. I pushed the thought away and approached Alex.

"Alex, I'm back! So, did you finish checking in?" I cheerfully asked.

"Yup, all done. What do you want to do now?" He looked at me, exhausted but excited. "Want to rest? Go on a tour? Eat?" He presented the options and left the choice to me.

"How about we rest for about an hour and then go on a tour, and during the tour, we eat?" I yawned to show my exhaustion but also to show him that it's okay to show you're exhausted in front of me. "What do you say, Mr Alex?" I drawled.

"Yeah, let's do that. We need some rest anyway," he said as he got up and held my tote bag for me. "Come on, follow me. I'll take you to your room." The concern that was shown when I had the attack during the flight has come back in his eyes. "Our rooms are a bit far from each other since they weren't able to find any connected empty rooms, but whatever you need, you can just call me through Botim. I'll answer in the first ring; I promise," he said, looking concerned.

"Don't worry, Alex. Nothing urgent will happen." We arrived at my room, and before I entered, I hugged Alex to comfort him. "So, we meet in 1 hour and 30 minutes, yeah? Exactly at 6:45 pm. Don't be late unless you have a death wish," I joked to reduce the tension in the air.

"I won't be late. You're the one who takes 2 hours to do makeup. Rest well!" he smiled. "Go in. I'll go to my room once you close your door." I smiled back and went into my room.

I, for a fact, know that I won't be able to take a nap after the symptoms I had earlier. I feel so horrified, as if , if I sleep, I won't wake up again. But there's one way to distract me from these thoughts: calling Anastasia. Indeed, Bali is 12 hours ahead of Boston, but Anastasia doesn't sleep on weekends until 7 or 8 am, so she should answer.

I connected to the hotel's Wi-Fi and called her. As expected, she answered after the second ring. "Avenue, hey, girl! What's up?"

"Ana! I was hoping you wouldn't answer. You need to fix your weekend sleep schedule; it's not healthy in the long run," I started as if I was the older one.

"Shut up, Avène. I'm older than you and majoring in psychology, so I know, but I'm also living life. I mean, what *is* life if you don't go clubbing looking for a lover?" She continued blabbering. "I mean, look at you, girl. You're in B A L I, and with whom? A guy who you can hit on. I know you guys see each other as siblings, but you can also be lovers. You know, he's ten times better than Nicholai! But anyway, I seriously need to find my man soon; I'm 23! I feel like a single grandma." Anastasia, the chatterbox, I knew that she would distract me from my thoughts by talking about the most bizarre topics.

"Ana, calm down. I'm not going to date Alex, and neither are you a grandma. You'll find your lover when it's the right time. Like, even I haven't found him yet." I felt sorrow and my throat tightening while saying this. I miss him.

"Yeah. How's Bali, though? And why aren't you resting when you just arrived?" There comes the questionnaire. Isabella and Anastasia are alike. I survived Isa's questionnaire last time, so I should survive this one, too.

"So far, it's good. We're planning to go on a tour in an hour, so I'm too excited to be resting; plus, I need to start getting ready soon. You know, I'm slow," I brightly said. "By the way, what should I wear? My dress? Skort? Shorts?" I asked to change the topic of the questions. "Oh, and I need to look sexy, so choose a sexy option. And no, I'm not going to look sexy for Alex; it's for Bali," I blurted before she replied.

"A dress, all girls look sexy in a dress. Oh my God, especially if you have a mini-one. Your thighs are built like the figure skater you are, so you should flex them. You're my inspiration to work out my thighs, except not on the ice," she said, sounding like a fan fawning over a celebrity.

To this day, I have no idea why Anastasia is obsessed with thighs. She says there are different types, and each type must match you to 'look' sexy. But in my opinion, everyone is sexy in their own way.

She says I have figure-skating thighs. Well, I have been a professional figure skater ever since I was five years old, and that's how I was inspired to be a sports journalist because I wanted to continue to talk to professional athletes and be attached to my sport even if I quit it, but now I'm forced to let it go.

"How about the white mini dress I wore on Cora's 19th birthday?" I asked as I searched for it. This dress is my favourite out of my entire collection. Nicholas was the one who gifted it to me on my 19th birthday, but that's only one of the reasons why it's my favourite. "I can wear it with my Samba shoes and my black tabby coach purse," I described the outfit for her so she could imagine how it would come out.

"Oh yes, chic, elegant woman. At this point, Alex will fall in love with you first," she fantasised.

"I'll slap you if you don't stop," I threatened. "Anyways, I'll go change now. Take care and go sleep, for God's sake," I begged, hopeful she'd listen this time.

"Yep, I'll do one final TikTok scroll! Enjoy, sexy," she made a kissing sound on the mic as a goodbye.

I put my phone down after I checked the time. It's now 5:30. I have exactly an hour left to get ready, trying my best to be fast so I prove Alex wrong.

"Avène, are you ready?" Alex whispers through the door while knocking.

"Yep, just give me one second, and I'll open the door!" I screamed as loud as possible so he could hear me over his loud knocks. I place my lipstick in my purse and head to the door to let him in before he breaks it with his knocks. "You like?" I spin around to show him my outfit.

"Wow, you look amazing. It's giving Bali vibes. Now, let's go," he sarcastically said, rushing me to get out of the room.

"Alex, that's so mean," I stopped in the hallway to go back and get my phone and medication in case of another symptom. "You're the worst. Don't do that to your future girlfriend; she'll break up with you right away. I'm not even joking," I returned the sarcasm. "I forgot my phone, wait by the elevator, I'll be right there."

"Okay, just hurry up!" he yelled so loudly that I almost thought someone would call security on him.

I grab my medicine and hide it in a specific mini pocket I have in my purse just in case Alex opens it for any reason; he won't see it. Next, I grab my phone and speed walk to Alex before he says, "See, I told you. You're slow as fuck." Except that instead of 'fuck,' he would say 'booger.' It cringes me all the time.

We find our tour guide standing with many other people near where we're supposed to get our minibus. "So, we're going on a group tour, not private?" I curiously ask Alex.

"Yeah, I thought you'd like it better that way," he nervously said, thinking he messed up the plans.

"Of course, I like it better this way! This was exactly why I asked. I thought that we all wait together now, but then we split up, which would be kinda sad. This is going to be fun!" I excitedly said while swinging around to see how many people were going with us.

"You scared me there. For a moment, I thought you wanted to do it privately," he confessed. "Come on, the bus is here," he grabbed my hand and took me with him to wait in the queue. But as I turned around to walk in the same direction as Alex, I'm not sure, but I think I saw a glimpse of Nicholas. This can't be possible, so it must be another symptom, right? Hallucination? But my doctor said they won't happen until I'm at the end-of-life stage. Maybe I just miss him.

Alex and I grab a seat, focusing our attention on the tour guide. "Welcome to Bali, everyone. My name is Wayan, and it pleases me to be the one to show you the beauty of Bali today. Since it's getting late and most of the attractions close around 7:30, we will visit Campuhan Ridge Walk. It's a lovely place filled with nature and romance in the air. You can easily find places to have dinner there, so don't worry about that. Please enjoy the ride."

"Romance in the air," Alex drawled. "I guess you and I are going to be forced to act romantic," he smirked while tapping my shoulder with despair.

"You've got to be kidding me," I look at his hand. "Take your funky hand off me, idiot." I push it away and grin.

"Yeah, I've just confirmed that I'd rather die than act romantic with you. I could *never*," he claimed.

"As if I asked you to be romantic," I mocked. "Piss off, Alex. Look at the nature outside your window instead of shoving your face in front of me." I gestured at the window to show him that he had so many more things to look at.

"Booger," he whispered in my ear, knowing damn well it'll make me slap him, which I did.

CHAPTER 12

Avène

We arrived at the Campuhan Ridge Walk, and I was speechless. I've never seen this sort of nature. It slightly reminds me of Georgia, but this place has art in its nature.

I stood there for a couple of minutes without talking, just taking in the beauty, and Alex understood without saying a word. I took some deep breaths, but I felt suffocated, wanting to cry. Thoughts on how unfair this world is came back to me when I realised I wouldn't be allowed to see this type of nature anymore. This is my last time.

I felt a teardrop on my lips, and it tasted like salt; tears and the ocean are all the same. I wiped my tears off and held Alex's hand to go catch up with the tour group. "Alex, tomorrow we should go to Bali Sea."

"Sounds lovely," he gently replied.

Although Alex and I argue most of the time, whenever I need him, he is always there for me. He knows when I'm hurting and when I'm not, when it's the proper time to joke and when it isn't. He's the brother I wished Denis would've been. I'm glad I chose to go on this trip with Alex.

"Alex, take a good professional picture of me standing here." I handed him my phone and went posing by the palm tree. "Take more than one. I need to impress my followers on Insta," I clarified before he messes up and ends up taking none.

I turn around to do another pose, and there he is. Six-foot tall, beautiful hazel eyes reminded me of the clear autumn sky, with golden brown skin glowing under the sun and broad shoulders making him look like a kingdom ruler. The nature surrounding him makes him look like the purest soul, with dazzling eyes glistening in the light. His outfit is as magical as he looks: perfectly tailored white linen pants and shirt. Alex calls out my name, and I unfortunately snap back to reality.

"Alex," I breathlessly say as I walk back to him.

"Yes?"

"You might think I'm out of my mind, but I just saw Nicholas," I declare while feeling my throat tightening again.

"What?" he sounded confused, looking around to spot him.

"Nicholas. He's here, I swear," I repeat myself.

"Are you hallucinating? Nicholas is in Boston, drowning in meetings," he looks around again. "If he is here, show me where he is."

I gesture towards the spot I saw him earlier, confident that he's still there. But he wasn't. "I swear Nicholas was there. He was wearing a linen white set. I'm not joking," I rushed out to make Alex believe me. "Even when you held my hand earlier to go on the minibus, I saw him, but I thought I was hallucinating. This time, I'm sure it was him; I swear." It can't be my symptoms, I'm sure of it. "I fear that he's also staying at our hotel, so if we don't see him here again, I'll find him in the hotel," I confidently said to Alex, making this my new mission in Bali.

"I hope you're right," Alex sounded concerned.

"I am going to be right," I claimed. I should probably focus on only enjoying my time in Bali with Alex as I have a feeling that the next time I see Nicholas, I might find something that would make me hate him more or wouldn't like, but at the same time, I'm longing for him. I want to see him again in case it's my last time.

CHAPTER 13
Nicholas

Sophia and I arrived in Bali within ten hours since we used my private jet. We spent our first day at Waterborn Bali, which Sophia enjoyed, but I didn't. It's such a hassle to go on the rides, although there was no queue since I rented the entire park.

Today is our second day here, and we just woke up to have a late breakfast before planning for the day. We quickly got ready and went down to the lobby, but Sophia realised that she hadn't put any lipstick on. She excused herself to go to the bathroom as I patiently waited for her by the piano placed in the hotel's entry. It reminds me of Avène, so I change my seat.

I heard a familiar voice, and as I turned around to confirm my suspicion, I couldn't believe that I was right; it was Alex. I don't approach him, and before he sees me, I get up and text Sophia to meet me at the buffet.

What is he doing here? Alone or with Avène? I know that Avène has wanted to come to Bali for the past ten years or so, but why not today out of all days?

What if she sees Sophia? I never wanted her to find out that I have a fiancée, and I hope it stays that way. I kept on thinking of who might accompany Alex other than Avène until my phone's screen lit.

Nicholas: *Meet me at the buffet.*

Sophia: *You seriously couldn't wait for 5 minutes?*

Nicholas: *I'm sorry, I couldn't find a seat in the lobby.*

Sophia: *Liar.*

Nicholas: *Liar?*

Did she seriously just call me a liar? I did lie, sure, but what gives her the right to say that, and how does she know I've lied?

"I know that you were lying, and I know exactly why," Sophia said while approaching me.

"What? Could you please elaborate?" I stuck to the formality that Anderson had given me lectures about.

"I know that you changed your seat because you saw Avène," she clarified all my suspicions.

So, Alex *is* here with Avène. "Avène is here?" I asked, confusedly, to show her that I hadn't seen her. "How'd you know?"

She sighed and said, "Nichol, don't play games with me. I know that you saw her in the lobby. She was with me in the bathroom; that's how I know she's here."

"Oh, makes sense. But I swear I didn't see her. I came here because I couldn't find a seat," I half honestly answered. She doesn't know that I saw Alex, and neither does she need to know.

"You don't look like you're lying, so fine, I'll believe you," Sophia sincerely said. "Let's forget about her and have breakfast before they close."

We didn't mention Avène anymore during breakfast; we spoke about plans, but most of the time, we ate in silence. Once we were done, we started planning for the day. We woke up quite late as we were exhausted from yesterday, so realistically, we can't plan much as it's already 4:30 PM. "How about we go for a swim at the pool for an hour and then change and go to Campuhan Ridge Walk? I heard that it's lovely there," I suggested.

"Yeah, sounds fun, but is that place aesthetically pleasing? I need something to post on Instagram." There she goes again, thinking of ways to showboat. This is the habit I hate the most in Sophia.

"Don't worry, you're going to be speechless when you see it," I assure her, although I would love to break her phone to never hear about her posts again.

We changed into our outfits after the one-hour swim. Sophia insisted on wearing matching couple clothes.

I was forced to wear my customised white linen set from Hermès while she wore her white dress from Chanel.

Once we finished getting ready, we headed to our limousine waiting for us next to a minibus where tourists who chose to go with a tour guide stood. Sophia was silent the entire time in the car, except for sometimes when she asked me to take pictures of her. With full honesty, I enjoy it when Sophia stays silent for a long period. But once we arrived at the place, she was bipolar opposite.

My friend who suggested this place did not disappoint; the view is staggering. "Sophia, let's go for a walk first; we can take pictures at the end," I suggested.

To my surprise, she didn't argue and agreed right away. "Okay, but when the sun is about to set, we need to take pictures. They are a necessity." Unfortunately, within five minutes, she insisted on taking those damn photos. I'm convinced she's mentally ill. "Come on, that's enough walking. Let's take photos now, make sure they are high quality."

"You've got to be shitting me," I muttered under my breath.

"I heard you. Don't use those filthy terms again," she advised. Coincidentally, every time I mutter a swear word, she hears it, no matter how far or near, so I don't know how she heard me when she was five metres away.

Using 'filthy terms' is not allowed in Patrick's family because they destroy the elegance that we are supposed to possess. But no one had heard Anderson use all sorts of filthy terms while murdering my mother except for me.

As we were taking pictures, I turned around and there she was. Five foot seven, blue eyes shining like sapphire, with a smile flickering across her face like a hologram. She looked like the most beautiful woman I've ever seen in my entire life, with a mini white dress making her look like a gorgeous butterfly, with wings filling in all nature. We made eye contact, and I was lost in her eyes, deeper than the ocean.

She looked dismayed once she saw me, and at that moment, I wanted to walk up to her and apologise for everything, even if it wasn't my fault. However, Sophia decided to stop taking photos and wanted to head back to have dinner at the hotel before calling it a day and ending it there.

I followed Sophia this time without arguing with her since I knew that the sooner we left, the less burden Avène would feel.

After around thirty minutes, we reached our hotel and headed straight for dinner. I stopped by the bathroom while Sophia went to the buffet. This led me to bump into Alex on the way to the restaurant.

There was a stretched moment of silence before any of us spoke. "Alex, what are you doing here?" I ask, although his Hawaiian-style outfit screams that he's here on vacation.

"I'm here to relax," he says nervously, looking around. "And you?" He examines my outfit for what he's looking for.

"Conference." Avène and Alex never knew that I had a fiancée. I always kept it hidden because I knew how much Avène would be hurting if she found out. Despite us sharing the same hotel right now, I hope Avène never finds out. "Anyone else with you?" I casually asked.

"No, just me," he lies, not knowing that I've seen Avène earlier, but I don't push him to tell me the truth.

"Okay, well, it's nice to see you again. I have to go," I excused myself before Sophia came looking for me or Avène showed up. As for my relationship with Alex, it has indeed changed a lot since the event that occurred eleven days ago. Alex and I used to sit for hours talking or hanging out and enjoying ourselves, no matter how busy I was or how busy he was. Now, we are simply just people who know each other and would talk for a maximum of five minutes.

I find Sophia sitting at a table that's in the VIP area, so there's no way Avène or Alex will come up here and see us. "What's on the menu today?" I ask without mentioning that I've seen Alex or Avène.

"International, but there are many Indonesian dishes you should try," she replies, pointing to where those dishes are.

"I'll get my food and come back, don't go anywhere," I command. The last thing I wanted on a trip I was forced to go to was something happening.

I get my food and come back to find the table empty. "You've got to be kidding me," I say, looking around for ginger hair and wearing a white dress. I think of places she might be since I didn't see her at the buffet or anywhere in the VIP area. The bathroom down in the reception comes to my mind, so I head there first.

As I reached the public area of the restaurant, I saw Avène and Alex sitting at a table. Unfortunately, I wanted to ignore them and move on with my search for Sophia, but Avène fixed her eye contact on me, looking shocked again, so I walked up to them.

I had only three steps left to reach their table when I felt a hand twisting me around, and before I knew who it might be, her mouth was on mine.

Fuck, Sophia.

CHAPTER 14
Avène

Thirty minutes later, we arrived at the hotel. I was exhausted, so I suggested to Alex to have dinner right away and then call it a day, so that we restore energy for tomorrow.

Alex had to use the bathroom, so I went ahead and got food till he caught up. So far, Bali is literal perfection. Everything is so calm and beautiful, and the people here are also sweet and helpful. But seeing Nicholas did make me feel uneasy, as I had planned never to see him again, yet I was longing for him.

I sat at a table, and after ten minutes, Alex caught up. We started discussing tomorrow's programme until I turned around and saw Nicholas again. It all happened so fast, but the ginger girl I saw earlier in the bathroom was behind and pulled him into a kiss.

A kiss.

I must be hallucinating again. There's no way Nicholas would allow a girl to kiss him; he hates dating, too. That's what he told me unless this is another hidden secret behind all the lies he had told.

I couldn't look at them anymore. I felt nauseous as if another symptom was coming up, so I got up and went to my room without explaining anything to Alex. I made it halfway through the hall before Nicholas stopped me. "Avène, I can explain," he desperately said.

I continued to walk, ignoring him. But he exceeded my pace and held my hand, forcing me to hear him out. The last thing I wanted from my final trip in my entire life was to see a sight like that or be in this situation. He knew I hadn't gotten over him this whole time, yet he lies through his teeth.

"Avène, please," he pleaded. "It'll take only a couple of minutes. Listen to my explanation and then decide." He softened his voice to try to convince me, so I decided to give him his final chance to explain himself ever again.

"Sophia is my fiancée. My father forced me to marry her. In our family, no one is allowed to stay single at the age of twenty-three. If I tell them I want you, not her, they will disown me, and you know exactly why," he lowered his voice, saying the last phrase. "I'm marrying her in two months. Once I do, I probably will never see you again. I do want to fight for you, Avène. I don't think I'll get a chance like this anymore to say this, but you are the most beautiful girl I've ever seen in my entire life. You aren't beautiful just by looks but personality-wise as well. I promise you, even with all the misunderstandings we had, you are my first and last love. I've never had feelings for Sophia and never will," he confessed, thinking I'd immediately forgive him.

Nicholas has never been good at explaining or conveying his emotions, so I am considerate. But this doesn't define his actions. If he wanted me, he would fight for me.

I pushed his hand away and continued to walk to my room without saying a word. I felt too breathless and dizzy to speak, probably another symptom of a panic attack. But as I tried to pick up the card to open my room, everything went black.

CHAPTER 15
Nicholas

I didn't think of how Sophia would react or what Anderson would say if he found out. I immediately ran after Avène.

I caught her by her hand in the hallway before she reached her room. For a second, I was concerned about her health since her hand felt oddly thinner than usual, but I brushed it off and spoke up before it was too late.

"Avène. I can explain," I desperately said. "Avène, please," I begged. "It'll take only a couple of minutes. Listen to my explanation and then decide," I said as if my life is on the line.

I've never been this desperate or careless in my life. I always took precautions, and whatever I wanted would easily come to me without me desperately begging and working hard for it until Avène. She's been digging a new side of me that I never knew about or saw when I was with Sophia. I didn't know how this conversation would go, as the previous one didn't go so well, but I confessed everything in summary.

Despite my explanation, she pushed my hand and continued to walk to her room. I confessed everything, so I didn't follow her to give her some space. I watched her pull her room card out from her purse, but before she achieved that, she collapsed in front of my eyes again.

At that moment, Sophia found me and kept calling out my name to get my attention, but the only person occupying my focus was Avène. I ran to her and left Sophia spectating from behind.

I place Avène on my lap to check if she is conscious and the severity of her panic attack, but I soon realise that she isn't breathing.

I perform CPR on her while yelling at Sophia to call 112. Although Sophia is burning with jealousy, she isn't that naive to ignore this situation and not do as I commanded her. Avène loses the arrives within seconds.

They took Avène, and I followed them shortly after, briefly explaining the situation to Alex. We're in Bali, and it's late at night. God knows how bad he would've reacted if he found out Avène wasn't in her room. Surprisingly, he was also understanding and reacted better than last time, even though this time her condition is worse for whatever reason, and I have a feeling partially isn't my fault.

Sophia went back to our room while Alex and I drove to the hospital. We arrived when Avène was able to breathe again and found the doctors running some more tests. After a couple of minutes, we found out something we never would have imagined.

Avène hasn't regained consciousness yet, so we sit in silence, stunned by the news. Never in a million years have I thought of losing Avène this soon. Yes, I knew I might never see her again, but I never thought she and I would never live on the same planet again. But that's not the worst part. The worst part is she knew she had Glioblastoma with only three months left to live, for God knows how long. I've never felt this horribly guilty feeling, even with the amount of people I've killed and harmed in the past; for the first time, I think it's making me feel like the weakest man alive.

"Nicholie, I don't feel so good," Alex says, breaking the silence. "I can't feel my hands or legs," he says, crying, looking at his hands and legs.

"What do you mean?" I say, concerned. Although Alex has always been babied and acted like a baby, he never complained when he was unwell emotionally or physically.

"I'm trying to wipe my tears and get up to ask doctors when I can see Avène, but I can't," he looks up at me pleading for help. "I can't move. Seriously." I briskly stood up and walked over to him.

"I'll try helping you stand up, okay? Use me as your crutch," I say, trying to help him stand up and walk, but he feels so heavy on my shoulders as if he completely lost the ability to hold himself up. "Come on, you can do it," I desperately try to make him stand up.

"Nicholie, I can't," he says.

"Come on, you can do it," I repeat.

"Nicholie," he repeats. I don't hear him.

"Stand up, Alex. Use my shoulder for support," I cheer again.

"Nicholas," he yells, bringing my focus back. "I can't. Put me down, please," he asks, still crying.

"I'll come back. I'll bring doctors, and they'll figure out what's going on. It'll be okay, I promise," I run to the reception and explain the situation. The nurse soon follows me with a wheelchair to escort Alex to a room so the doctors can examine him.

"Nicholie, but I can't leave Avène alone," he refuses the wheelchair.

"We will come back to her once you're okay. She'll get worried if she sees you like this. Get healthy for her sake, please," he doesn't say another word and accepts the wheelchair.

After an hour of examination, the doctors soon informed me that Alex was temporarily paralysed as he couldn't accept the news about Avène. I'm glad it's only temporary, but they said it could take months for him to heal, depending on his mental acceptance. I didn't expect my day to be full of shock and despair. If only the dawn of love did not exist.

CHAPTER 16
Avène

"Davai, Davai!" Coach Novikov cheered as I got into position to attempt my triple toe loop.

It's my second on-ice practice today, and so far, I've been training for 10 hours due to having ballet, off-ice, dance, and on-ice classes. Lately, I've been struggling with my triple toe loop for some reason; although I go by "The Russian Rocket dupe," Alexandra Trusova will always be the original. I don't know if it's the idea of mocks coming up and making it hard for me to focus or if it's my body giving up on me at 16.

Coach Mark Novikov has been with me ever since I started my figure-skating journey at the age of 5. I could never express how grateful I am to have him. Without him, I wouldn't be a silver national medallist at fifteen or a gold international medallist at sixteen. Although Coach Novikov is a perfect coach to have, I hate all the times he would get mad when I couldn't land a jump, element, or spin with proper technique, such as now.

Times like these make me rethink my entire decision of wanting to be a figure skater who reaches the Olympics. Pressure from family, friends, teachers, coaches, and media. It may seem so easily achieved to many, but the backstage broke even the original Russian rocket.

Just like ballet, I used to do gymnastics to increase my strength, balance, and flexibility. After 3 years, I removed it from my routine as the coach became too aggressive whenever I wouldn't achieve a skill. I love gymnastics as the second alternate sport, and I wanted to continue to be great at it until I can compete, but unfortunately, that goal is just a dream now.

"Zdorova, Avène," Coach says, bringing my focus back to him. "This is what I wanted. Spasibo!" He hugs me, and at that moment, I realise I have finally landed my triple toe loop.

"Coach, I want to quit figure-skating." Everyone falls silent.

"Yeah, sure, you always keep on saying that whenever something like this happens," he laughs, shaking my shoulder as if I meant it as a joke this time too.

"I'm serious. I'm quitting," I say with a serious tone I've never used with him in the entire 11 years he's been with me.

"You're serious?" he looks around, speechless. "What will your parents say?" he gradually started to raise his voice. "They spent thousands on you, and you want to throw all that away?"

"Stop guilt-tripping me," I say, pushing his hand off my shoulder. "I'll deal with my parents, don't worry," I snap back at him. "I'll miss you, and I know I might regret this sometime later, but it's time for me to do something for *me*, not for people around me." I skate out without celebrating my achievement, as it doesn't matter anymore.

I take off my skates to go back home, but I suddenly pass out. The next thing I know when I open my eyes is that I'm at the hospital looking like a 21-year-old, not sixteen. It took me a few blinks until I remembered the reason I was in the hospital.

Conversation with Nicholas led me here again, meaning I was having a flashback of the day I quit figure-skating. The last time I had a flashback of my brother's tantrum was when I was 15. I aged by one this time. And unlike last time, I found only a letter placed near to me, no Alex, no Nicholas.

I straightened up to open the letter, but as I did, a doctor came in. "How are you feeling, Ms. Avène?"

I look up and reply, "Okay." The doctor takes in a deep breath, the same way the other doctor did to inform me about my illness, so I quickly speak before she says it. "I know; I have Glioblastoma with only three months left to live."

"You knew. But decided to hide it from the two gentlemen?" Her question worries me as it makes me feel like she told them everything about my illness.

"Yes, I knew, and I didn't tell anyone, so I die in peace without hurting them. Please don't tell me you told them." I sigh, feeling my eyes wanting to water.

"Unfortunately for you, I did, but fortunately for me, I now know that my patient isn't suffering alone," she says as she comes to me for a hug. "I know just from the test results that you had so many symptoms affecting your daily life to the extent that you had to drink symptom relief pills. Don't hide anymore, my dear," she leaves me speechless in my quiet room with a letter in my hand.

I snap out of it and open the letter.

"Dear Avene,

If you are reading this letter, you are probably wondering where Alex and I are; if not me, it is surely Alex.

Alex is okay, busy with some things, but he'll check on you soon. We both know that you are ill, and we know it's Glioblastoma. I know why you hid this from all of us, but to clear that thought out of your head, we aren't suffering because of you, and none of this is because of you. Life is just simply unfair, and we live to fight against it. We are all here to support you, just like you always supported us.

I'm not there with you right now because I don't want your health to worsen, and I'm sure you don't want to see me either. I'll do as you say, but please know that I don't have any feelings for Sophia.

I've never said this to you, and I truly do regret it, but at the age of five, when my mother passed away, that taught me that the things you love can be gone in an instant. I never loved or allowed anyone to get close to me ever since. But then I met you.

The day I did not fight back for you was because I realised I was madly in love with you, and today, I realise life is temporary. So, if death does us part, I'll fight to find you in the next. Even if you might hate me now, I will fight for you. I will fight to get lost in those beautiful eyes that shine every day like sapphire. I will fight to see your smile that winks love at me.

My love, the war starts today."

I put the letter down and started sobbing until that was the only thing I started hearing in my room. I never thought Nicholas would confess in this lifetime. Never in the entire seven years have I been delusional enough to imagine a scenario like this.

Nicholas confesses all this when I don't have much time left on my hands. Could it be a pity? Could he be playing me again so he doesn't seem like the bad guy in this story? Could what he wrote be true?

"Nicholas confessed," I say out loud, to see how it sounds, and start laughing maniacally when I realise it sounds like a sad ending in an American movie.

Did he say all that without thinking about how we won't seem like a normal couple out there? Is he about to start a war without my permission? I never said I still love him. Yes, I reacted strangely and disliked the idea of him kissing his fiancée, but that doesn't mean he can assume I love him.

Even if I haven't gotten over him, he knows better than anyone that he can't easily win against his father after all these years. He might lose his job just because of me, me, a person who will be a memory either way.

I disliked this decision he took, so I stood up, fighting through the pain to go and stop him. "Ms Avène, where are you going?" the nurse at the reception asked, looking concerned.

"I feel okay now. I need to leave," I declared and continued to head towards the exit.

I hurry to reach Nicholas. Although I don't know his room number, I'll find him somehow. Even if I'm supposed to hate him, I won't leave him in a home without heart.

CHAPTER 17
Nicholas

"Alex, I get it now," I say after a stretched silence between me and Alex.

"You get what?" he looks at me, confused by what I just said.

"I get what I should do," I sigh, preparing myself for a conversation I never had before. "I know I should've done this a long time ago, but now I'm ready for it," I declare. "Listen to what I say carefully, yeah?"

"I'll listen," he assures me.

"When I was five years old, as you know, my mother died. But what you don't know is that she was murdered by my father. He murdered her for spending so much money on curing her Parkinson's disease, which she developed from the shock of finding out my father cheated on her. Ever since then, I made a promise to myself that I would take revenge on my father, whom I call Anderson whenever I'm alone. I also made another promise to myself to not love or let anyone get close to me because that event taught me that the things you love will always be temporary. When I met you, I couldn't resist you. I wanted you to be the best friend I never got to experience. I admit most of the time, I'm cold to you, but that's only because of my past. Otherwise, I'm worrying about you right now as you lay on this bed. The same goes for Avène, my fiancée you saw me with. She was forced on me by Anderson; I never had feelings for her. You might find this unbelievable, but since the day I saw Avène, I fell in love with her. Based on what I previously mentioned, you know why I never fought back for her. Otherwise, she'll always be my first and last love." I take a deep breath and continue, "Knowing about her illness made me realise how much of a weakling I was, even with all the power in my hands. She and I might not have much time anymore in this lifetime, but I promise to still fight for her now, and I'll fight again and again in each lifetime," I announce.

"Wow," he says, not knowing what to say next. "Is this a new American movie?" he jokes. "Listen, I always knew behind that tough-looking face and posture of yours is you that needs help from others. I just never said anything because I knew you wouldn't admit it, and I knew although you have been hurting Avène, you didn't mean to. That's why I never snapped at you, except for last time, and I'm sorry for that." He sounds mature for the first time in a while. "So, what's the plan now?"

"I need to finish off Anderson first while finding a way to tell Avène about your paralysis before she sees you. Then I get rid of Sophia and fight Avène to accept me," I state, leaving out the part about how I'm going to finish off Anderson. "And you, focus on getting better. I'll keep checking on you via call or text; my flight back to Boston is tomorrow."

"Okay, got it," he says with a thumbs up. "Stay safe."

"The way you are being so mature today is imaginary," I joked.

"Go away, booger," we laughed before I left.

I dropped a letter by Avène's room to give her a brief plan layout before she woke up looking for Alex. After I've done that, I immediately headed to the hotel to plan something with Sophia before she goes and tells Anderson what's going on.

CHAPTER 18
Avène

"Room 1087," the receptionist announced after forty minutes of begging him to share the information with me. I thank him and go to the nearest elevator I can find.

I reached his room, but I kept hesitating to ring their doorbell. So many thoughts and questions have been coming up in my brain. What if she's in there with him? What if they are busy making out because all that he told me was a lie? What if he has already ruined his life? What if his fiancée makes fun of me after finding out I'm ill?

I kept staring at the door, and when I was about to leave, I started hearing screams from inside. I got worried, so I couldn't stop myself from eavesdropping.

"So, you knew and decided not to tell me anything?" Nicholas yells first.

"Yes, because that bitch always occupies your life," Sophia raised her voice over Nicholas.

"So, you do know how to swear," he states. "And how did that breakfast taste after knowing you might've ruined someone's life?" Nicholas asks. "Because I hope it gives you the worst illness of your life soon," he emotionlessly says.

I've never heard Nicholas raise his voice before. He always got what he wanted, and if someone dared to hurt him, he would get revenge in a way I don't want to think about.

"These are your true colours, after all, Nicholas," Sophia says, sounding upset. "Exactly why I didn't want to tell you I've seen her take medication in the bathroom and why I was contemplating the idea of calling an ambulance for her." Sophia is the real bitch now. "I wish the doctors failed to save her, like how your CPR failed on her."

"When we go back to Boston, make sure to leave right away. I'll let father know about your true self. I recorded our entire conversation." I felt proud hearing Nicholas achieve the first stage of this war, but at the same time, I felt awful. I'm dying anyway; why fight for me?

I left after I made sure that Sophia had accepted defeat. I reach my hotel room and collapse on the bed, exhausted from the pain in my chest, but I don't allow myself to rest just yet. I must text Nicholas before he does something he'll regret.

Avene: *Hi Nicholas, I've read your letter and overheard your conversation with Sophia, so I decided to text you this. I'm okay, so don't come looking for me, but you must stop this war you're about to start. I'm dying anyway in less than three months; throwing away your entire life for me when I'm dying so soon isn't worth it and not something I'll allow you to do. Thank you for confessing your love for me; it means a lot, but please move on and continue to live as if you hate me. It's for the best.*

Nicholas: *Can I see you now? There's something important I need to tell you.*

Avène: *Come to my room in the hotel.*

Nicholas: *Coming.*

I wait for him while I try to hide the fact that I'm in pain as much as possible. After around three minutes, I heard him knocking, so I let him in. "Avène, I'm glad you're okay."

"Yeah, thanks to you," I awkwardly say. We haven't had a face-to-face conversation in over seven months, which makes this feel as awkward as possible.

"Okay, listen, I'll be quick." I nod at him. "Alex and I have planned this together, so you must trust us. I'm not throwing my life away; I'm doing this for you and myself. I need to live free." He doesn't sound like he will get convinced if I repeat myself. "Don't worry, but Alex isn't with us right now because he is temporarily paralysed." He throws at me the news with no signal.

"What."

"Don't worry. I promise he's okay. He was in shock after he heard about your illness, and the doctors say once he accepts the news, he will gradually regain his ability to move his hands and walk. It might take days, months, or years, but he'll get there," he explains to assure me that Alex is safe. But the pain in my chest, I can no longer hide. "What's wrong?"

"I've had this pain in my chest since I left the hospital," I say, as the pain further increases.

"You weren't discharged by the doctors, were you? Did you come straight to me right away after you woke up?" he asks, worried about what my answer will be.

"Yes, I came straight to you. I couldn't let you ruin your life like I did. No parents, no siblings, a home without—" I end up collapsing on his chest, so my next two words get muffled, "—a heart." He doesn't push me away; instead, he holds me in a tight hug, giving me the comfort I need.

"I miss hugging you, my love. We last did this in high school during a crisis." He takes us towards my bed and allows us to cuddle in the hope that the pain will ease. I listen to his heart, beating like a wild animal trying to escape his chest. Supposedly, it should annoy me, but for some reason, it brought me comfort, like when a baby drinks milk from the mother's breast.

We stay in comfortable silence, with so many words hanging in the air. I'm starting to feel exhausted after such a stressful day, so I decided to say what I must do before I pass out.

"Nicholas," I finally break the silence.

"Hmm?" he gently says, while his heart is doing the opposite, roaring like a lion.

"Thank you, and I'm sorry," I confess.

"If there's one person who should thank and apologise to the other, it's me, not you. Thank you for accepting me, and sorry for making you suffer alone," he continues to speak, but I gradually stop hearing him as I get too comfortable in my sleep. I would love to keep hearing his voice longer since I don't have much time left to enjoy it, but my exhaustion overpowers my passion.

CHAPTER 19
Nicholas

When I saw Avène's text, I didn't care anymore about whatever bullshit Sophia might be planning. I immediately took my hotel card and headed straight to Avène's room. She did say she was okay in her message, but that's Avène's nature; she would take a gunshot even for her worst enemy.

I knocked without hesitation once I reached her room, and thankfully, she let me in right away. I was so lost in my worry for her that I didn't know what to say. "Avène, I'm glad you're okay," is the only thing that I was able to say, although she was as pale as a clear sky.

"Yes, thanks to you," her response was more confusing than the weird feeling I'm feeling right now. I did save her life by taking her to the hospital, but I'm also partially the reason she had to experience that. I wanted to correct her and say she wasn't supposed to be thanking me, but I decided to take the safest route and move on.

I didn't know how to break the news to her. I hesitated for far too long, to the extent that the silence got awkward. "Okay, listen, I'll be quick." She nods at me for reassurance, but I still feel worried. "Alex and I have planned this together, so you must trust us. I'm not throwing my life away; I'm doing this for you and myself. I need to live free." I know that she probably wants to stop me again from 'throwing' my life away, but I refuse for that to happen. "Don't worry, but Alex isn't with us right now because he is temporarily paralysed."

I knew I messed up the way I said it the minute she said, "What?"

"Don't worry. I promise he's okay. He was in shock after he heard about your illness, and the doctors say once he accepts the news, he will gradually regain his ability to move his hands and walk. It might take days, months, or years, but he'll get there," I say before she stresses out. Ever since I came into her room, she looks like she's in pain but hiding it. After some moments of silence, that pain wasn't suppressed anymore. "What's wrong?"

"I've had this pain in my chest since I left the hospital," she explains, and then it all makes sense to me how she overheard Sophia and my conversation.

"You weren't discharged by the doctors, were you? Did you come straight to me right away after you woke up?" I worriedly said, afraid to hear her response.

"Yes, I came straight to you. I couldn't let you ruin your life like I did. No parents, no siblings, a home without—" She collapsed on my chest. At that moment, a part of me wanted to rush her to the hospital, but the other selfish part wanted to stay in this moment for a lifetime. "—a heart," she continued, although her words got muffled as I tightened my grip on her, giving both of us the comfort we needed.

I forgot how soft and vulnerable she felt until now. "I miss hugging you, my love. We last did this in high school during a crisis," I said. As I felt a rush of adrenaline, I brought us towards her bed to lie on it; at least her pain faded away.

We stayed in comfortable recovery silence for a while until she broke it by calling out my name. "Nicholas,"

"Hmm?" I gently say not to hurt her in any possible way.

"Thank you, and I'm sorry," she says after taking a long, deep breath.

"If there's one person who should thank and apologise to the other, it's me, not you. Thank you for accepting me, and sorry for making you suffer alone," I confess. "I'm sorry I couldn't chase you around sooner; things could've been different. I've always seen you as a valuable person in my life; that's why I tried to protect you in my way, not knowing it would've made you suffer to this extent. I promise in every life, I'll find you and treat you better, my love."

I wait for her response, but I look down and realise she's fast asleep. I place her comfortably on her pillow so that I can get up and go back to Sophia before she causes any chaos. "I'm sorry, my love. I'll come back when I'm a victor." I place a kiss on her forehead and leave.

CHAPTER 20
Avène

It's been three days since we returned from Bali, five days since chaos broke out, and four days since I last heard from Nicholas. The next morning, after Nicholas told me about Alex's diagnosis, I rushed to the hospital to check on him and couldn't forgive myself for forgetting about him and sleeping the night away.

He indeed was paralysed from his legs and hands, which broke my heart, and I couldn't resist my tears seeing him in that condition. I assured him that he'd be okay, and I'd help him go back to normal, and how we'd go to theme parks and do all the cool things we've always done for hours. I completely forgot I was the one that's dying.

During those entire two days we had left, I did not go on a tour or do whatever good stuff tourists are supposed to do in Bali. I spent them cooking for Alex, checking up on him, and taking him out to get some fresh air. Other times, when I was completely alone, I spent them crying, wanting to hold onto life, worrying about everyone, and sleeping. The one thing

I'm thankful for is that there have been no symptoms throughout the last couple of days.

Currently, I'm about to meet with the girls, but I can't stop looking at my bucket list. I know I should tick off Bali since I've been there not so long ago, but I also barely did anything there, except for the Campuhan Ridge Walk. I also know better than anyone that there's no way I will be able to go there again.

I took a last look at the bucket list before I forced myself to go and order an Uber. I'm usually never late, except for the one time with Isabella, which got her very suspicious. It can't happen again.

After around forty minutes, I arrived at Eleanor's mansion. That's right, the wanna-be Kylie Jenner 2.0 businesswoman is a rich girl. Eleanor's father is an owner of an investment company, which makes them millionaires. Eleanor and I are considered the rich girls of our friend group because, unlike Eleanor's father, mine owns a business but barely gives my brother or me any of those shares. Whenever I would ask him why, his answer would be, "Because I want to save up for retirement." My brother. I forgot about him up till now.

My brother and I had a hard time bonding in high school due to many factors. Because of that, he had tantrums and many difficulties that my parents tried to handle but couldn't. As those difficulties worsened, I would develop mental illnesses such as depression, anxiety, post-traumatic disorder, and so on. I also stopped taking care of myself, which led my parents to choose who to take care of first. They always chose my brother until I developed severe depression. They treated me like the most valuable thing in this world for the first time and cared about my safety. However, after three months, when I finally started healing, they lost interest in me again. Even when I developed anorexia from figure-skating, they never cared.

However, when I reached university, my parents started caring only about themselves. They forgot about Denis, too. That was the time when I was so thankful for being independent, for writing my book and for working all sorts of jobs to save up money. I brought Denis near me in Boston; he stays at a mental hospital where they take care of him and do everything he ever asks or wishes for while I focus on my studies. I was planning to let him live with me once I get a job, but now that I think of it, who will even care for him when I'm gone? No one knows I'm dying except for Alex and Nicholas, and no one other than Alex, Nicholas, and my friends know that he's in the hospital, but not which. I would love to ask Alex or Nicholas to take care of him, but Alex is ill, and Nicholas is probably in a tough position.

Although I never showed it, I love Denis. He's my brother, after all, and it's not his fault for being mentally ill, just like how it's not my fault for dying so soon. The funny thing is, I've always been afraid to develop any cancer, and now it's the reason I'm dying.

I brush off all the overthinking going on and bring my focus to Evelyn, who arrived at the same time as me. As expected of her, she breaks into a run and hugs me tightly, to the extent that I can't breathe. "Evelyn, calm down, girl."

"So, you don't like my hugs?" she says with fake cries.

"I do, but you knocked the air out of me. Chillax," I say, hopeful she'll get my point.

"So, you don't miss me?"

"I do, Evelyn. I miss you. I'm just saying, you almost killed me," I assure her.

"Fine," she acts mad and loses her grip on me.

"Hey, Eve, want me to hug you like you did?" I suggest not making her sad after we just met.

"Yes, ma'am. I have better resistance," she cheerfully says, forgetting that she's supposed to act mad.

I do it and realise even my physical abilities are not as they were before. "Did I choke you enough?" I ask although I know that was nothing compared to how she did it.

"Sure, yeah," she sarcastically says. "Come on, let's go to Eleanor." She grabs my hand and takes me with her.

We end up gossiping about Nicholas and Alex for two hours. Of course, I leave out the part that I'm sick and the reason why Alex is paralysed. The other two hours are spent gossiping about Cora's fiancé, who is soon-to-be her husband. The final three hours are spent swearing at Eleanor's sixth boyfriend, fighting with Isabella, and being delusional together. These were the best 7 hours I've had in a while; they were completely stress-free, and I could speak my heart partially honestly.

It's getting late, so I bid my farewell to them and leave in an Uber after having an entire twenty-minute argument with Eleanor to not force me to use her driver. I reach my house and immediately head to my room to sleep. After yapping so much, I can sleep for two entire days, but that soon changes when I receive a message on my phone.

CHAPTER 21
Nicholas

FOUR DAYS AGO

By the time I landed in Boston, I had finished preparing everything that I could need to finish off Anderson without the public knowing I was behind it.

I made Sophia stick to me and act like we were completely fine until I got what I wanted, although we had a horrible last day in Bali. We both headed home, but once we arrived, I didn't waste a single minute to go see Anderson.

I made sure Sophia was locked in our room and went knocking at Anderson's office. "Father, I've arrived," I announced.

"Please, come in," he replies. I open the door and go in, waiting for him to gesture for me to have a seat. "How was Bali, son?" he gestures for me to sit across from him.

"It was marvellous, beautiful nature out there," I casually say. "How have your days been?" I ask carefully.

"Hectic as usual, but met wonderful ladies last night at Elysium," he said as if it's something to be proud of.

"Delightful news. Anyways, I want to go rest for a bit before I head to work, but do you, by any chance, have time tonight to have dinner with me?" I ask, knowing he won't realise that after all these years, I never asked him to eat somewhere with me until today.

"Yes, of course we can. Let's do it at 8 PM," I agree and leave the room, heading back to Sophia.

"Sophia, listen to me carefully because I won't repeat myself twice," I advise. "I'll be busy tonight, so I can't come back home and have my farewells with you. Thankfully, by 9 PM, get out of this house. And whoever asks you why we broke up, say we just realised we weren't meant for each other. If you tell the truth, I'll show them what you said in the recording. Got it?" I command, not caring about being a gentleman in front of a piece of shit like her.

"Yeah," she nervously says.

"We're good, then." I smile and leave the room, heading to my office.

It's 8:30 PM, and Anderson and I have just arrived at the restaurant I reserved. We could have gone to Elysium and dined there, but Anderson had a special gift coming from me, so I had to book the entire restaurant.

"Please have a seat, father," I gesture for him as I sit across from him. "Ostra is famous for their Mediterranean seafood, so you should focus on ordering that," I state, watching the way he'll react in depth.

"Very well, then, I'll leave the ordering up to you," he suggests, making my plan easily work.

I gesture at the so-called 'waitress' to take our order before I start to become impatient. She comes over, and I order '*the regular.*'

Anderson and I ended up having a conversation about our business until our food came. On the table, we had the entire caviar selections, salt crust branzino, broiled lobster, and steaks in case Anderson gets picky. Beverages, nothing too fancy; Anderson has "Maiden Sway," and I got a cocktail with a name that matches the mood of today: "Count me in."

We ate in silence, and once Anderson finished his cocktail, I decided to stop acting and speak up before my plan was successful. "Anderson," he looks up at me, partially furious and partially curious. "Wishing you could punish me for that right now, am I right?" I continue without allowing him to answer, "Well, no need for that; you're dying anyways," I check my watch. "In about five minutes from now."

"What?" he looks at me, completely stunned by the mood switch.

"OH, you haven't realised yet?" I mocked, "No way, man. Seriously?" He looks more furious now than before. It's getting my adrenaline worked up. "Did you not realise how weird it is that I asked you to come to have dinner with me, although I haven't given you that offer ever in the past years?"

"What?" he repeats.

"God. You're a fucker, after all." I laugh when I see him being shocked, hearing me swear for the first time in front of his face. "You're the one person I'll never regret killing. Congrats on getting on my list." I take a deep breath and continue, ignoring how he is looking at me. "Listen to my monologue now. I'll stop messing around with you. I can't let you die without hearing what I've been waiting to say for ages." I start the monologue, not caring whether he wants to hear it or not. "First off, I know that you are a murderer just like me, except that you killed only my mother, or maybe more, who knows? I eventually found out. You don't need to know how or when, but anyways, I know that you swore at her while stabbing her, so the rules that you created for me and whoever came into our household are shit, just like you. Secondly, Sophia, who you said must be my wife in two months, hates to break it to you, but she has already left the house." I check my watch. "Yeah, man, it's 9 PM. Anyways, she is a bitch. She hurt Avène in Bali by swearing at her and all that. And when you die, I'm getting back to Avène. I'll tell you all about the good times with her when I follow you to hell. Oh, and before I forget, in 45 seconds, you should start to feel pain killing you."

"You planned all this? Why did you put up with me all these years if you hate me this much?" he asks as if something could change if I told him the answer.

"Yes, I planned all this. I didn't take you to Elysium, so no one knows about this. And no, the 'workers' in this restaurant are the people who work for me to get dirty work like this done; that's why I rented this restaurant for today. The public will see your cause of death as a heart attack; sounds familiar to mothers, doesn't it?" I look at his eyes deeper than before to make him remember the look on my face before his death. "I put up with you all these years so that you don't throw me into hell while you live a great life. I waited until I had enough power and passion to kill you in this pitiful way." He starts to groan as the pain kicks in from the poison I had put in his drink.

"You were after the money, motherfucker. I didn't raise you this way," he says in pain.

"I was after having a good life, so shut it and die quietly."

"I'll see you in hell," these were his last words before I saw him choke to death.

I left him like that while I let my workers hide all the evidence of any suspicious intake the police might find and gave them the approval to call 911 as if it was a nice, casual day for him.

I went back home and drowned myself in alcohol, waiting for a call from the police instead of texting Avène or Alex since it was still too risky for them to come into my life.

CHAPTER 22
Nicholas

NOW

After three days of interviews and exhausting questioning, it has finally come to an end. Tonight, the news will announce that Anderson is deceased due to a heart attack, and everything he has possibly owned is mine, including Elysium. His funeral will also be held tonight, but I won't be attending that until I check on Avène and Alex.

Nicholas: *Steps one and two of this war are done.*

Nicholas: *Anderson and Sophia are done.*

Avène: *I don't think I want to know how they are done, right?*

Nicholas: *Yeah, you don't. Don't open the TV at all today.*

Avene: *Okay?*

Nicholas: *Can I come and see you? I miss you, my love.*

I waited for her response, but I was left on seen for whatever reason. It didn't sit right with me, so I took my car and drove to her house. I tried calling her on the way there, but there was no response. I drove as fast as I could, afraid I'd be too late.

I reach her door and knock. Surprisingly, she opens it right away, but when she realises it's me, she wants to immediately close the door. It was at that moment that I realised she heard the news somehow. "I can explain."

"You did it, didn't you?" she nervously asks, hiding behind the door.

"I planned it, but I didn't do it." It's technically true. I planned it, but I didn't put the poison in his drink. They are my people who did it, but that still makes it not me who did it.

"Improvise. If you planned it, how did he die of a heart attack out of nowhere?" she asks, cracking this case open.

I can't help but say, "That's my girl," most proudly, but I hold back. "You don't want me to improvise, but I got revenge for me and you. You are mine now, my love," I say, afraid of how she'll react next.

"Fine, I'll believe you. I'm dying anyways, so it doesn't matter." It gives my heart this weird, hurting feeling every time I hear her thinking so lowly of her life, waiting for her time.

"Come here, love." I open my arms for her in the hope it'll give her any kind of comfort to not say things like that to herself. She comes, and I tighten my grip on her to let her know that she should just stay with me in the present. “My love, you know how that turtle from Kung Fu Panda says, ‘Yesterday is history, tomorrow is a mystery, but today is a gift. That’s why it’s called the present’?”

“Yeah?” she says, confused as to what my point is.

“He’s right. Livc only in the present with me, like we are unwrapping the gift together. From now on, don’t think about the past or the future. What happened has happened; we can’t change it, and what’s about to happen will happen. It could be changed depending on how we live today,” I say, kissing her on the forehead.

“Please never give grown-up quotes again; you sounded like a grandpa,” she sarcastically says to change the topic. But when she sees I’m serious, she replies on topic. “Yeah, okay. I’ll live in the present with you, unwrapping the gift.”

“Thank you.” I hug her and remind myself that, to decrease the risk of chaos’s sake, I must attend the funeral, although I wish I could stay with her here all night long. “Listen, I have to go to the funeral against my will, but wanna have our first date after tomorrow?” I ask before I go.

“I’m free.”

“Perfect, I’ll pick you up at 1 PM,” I leave her house happy, like a boy who bought new Deadpool merch.

CHAPTER 23
Avène

Before yesterday, Nicholas asked me to go on a date with him, and today is the day. After he left my house that day, I texted Cora, who had informed me about Nicholas's late father passing away. I didn't want to believe it, as I knew it had Nicholas involved somehow. That's why I was too scared to open the door for him. There's a saying: a person who steals once can steal forever more, and murder is like theft.

I don't know what he had done to Sophia. No one has heard from her for the last couple of days, and Nicholas hasn't been mentioning her at all. It makes me nervous when I think about all this, but I choose to trust him this one time.

Cora is against my date with him today, but she still came over to help me look like a girl he would never want to take his eyes off. So far, we are done with skincare and makeup. We are onto the hair now, thinking about a half up, half down with a blowout. It's the only thing we can do within the one-hour we have left.

I feel vulnerable today, and I want this moment to be something I'll remember in my final moments, so I choose to wear the most expensive outfit I own: a Prada sable dress, my Hermès Oran sandals, and my favourite coach tabby purse.

My father bought me this outfit when I graduated high school as a 'good luck' for a university present. Supposedly, parents and children always stay in contact after gifting such a thing, but in my case, they gifted me this present to say, "We did what we had to, now piss off." The next gift I'll receive will surely be at my funeral, and I can bet on that.

"Did he tell you where he'll be taking you?" Cora asks, stopping me from overthinking.

"Nope, didn't give me a single clue," I chuckle when I hear her gasp at my response.

"Damn. When Caleb took me on our first date, well, it was a surprise, but he gave me a hint of what vibes the date would be based on my outfit," she says, sounding concerned about this date more than me.

"Yeah, that's Caleb, though. This one is Nicholas. A guy who doesn't have experience with his actual love, only his fake one," I joke around to make Cora worry less. "Like, what's the worst thing that could happen?"

"Him burying you alive," she tickles my neck to create tension.

"Woah there. Get your fingers off me before I call your fiancée, who's my number one enemy, and bury you both alive," I threaten her. Her fiancée and I had this enemy thing going on ever since before they started dating in high school, but when they dated, it got worse because he would steal her away from me most of the time – unacceptable.

"Okay, we'll see about that." Now, go put on your dress so that I can style your hair.

"Sure," I halfway reach my room before she disturbs me again by announcing that Nicholas sent me a message.

"Wait, stop, come back," she yells.

"What is it now?" I ask, startled.

"Nicholas. He sent you a message," she announces, and I rush back to my phone.

Nicholas: *Hey, love. I'll be there in 40 minutes!*

Avène: *Can't wait ☺*

"OH. MY. GOD. Did you just flirt with him?" she asks, not allowing me to answer. "I can't wait to tell the girls," she cheerfully says. "Now, go continue getting ready." I go, but this time I take my phone with me to not get delayed.

GORLIESS:, *Group Chat*

Cora: *Guys, it's crazy. Nicholas and Avene aren't only going on their first date; they are flirting. They might unleash orgasms tonight!*

"Cora," I yell to make her stop fantasising about false dirt. "No one will be unleashing orgasms today or ever," I state. "Now put your phone down and go get all the things we are gonna need to style my hair. Or else."

"Wait, let me say one last thing to the group," she says, not listening to my threat.

"Okay, then. Let me also say something to someone."

Third-wheeling forever: *Group chat*

Avène: *Make sure you give your fiancée a wave of orgasms tonight because she's falsely fantasising about my soon-to-be boyfriend.*

"Avène, no, please delete it," she yells, rushing to my room and begging.

"Then stop texting the group your dirty thoughts because it won't happen, ever." I am telling the truth. I don't want Nicholas to be a sex toy; I want him to have meaning in my life.

"Ever? Why?" she asks, confused. "What if you get married and want to have kids? Will you adopt?"

"I'll adopt. Now get out, please. I'm still changing." I smile at her as I guide her from her shoulders to the door.

"Come out in ten minutes so I can do your hair." I nod and close my door. I feel a rush of emotions rising up my throat, but I swallow them down for the sake of my well-applied makeup.

CHAPTER 24
AvèNe & Nicholas

AVENE

Five minutes ago, Nicholas sent me a message that he was waiting for me in the lobby of my apartment. I look at myself for the sixth time now to make sure I look flawless, despite Cora ensuring me that I do.

"Come on, don't let the poor guy keep on waiting for you," she pushes me away from the mirror and takes me to the elevator.

"Yeah, let me check. Just one more thing," I say, opening my purse and making sure that I've put my medication in, just in case. "Okay, I'm done checking. I'm ready now."

"Have fun, babes. Tell me all about it later," she sweetly says. Cora is a sweet girl who gives advice and all the stuff a girl could need for help, but then, like any other friendship, there are times when she's so annoying.

"Thanks, girly," I hug her before I head down to Nicholas.

I reach the lobby, and when I look up to search for him, I immediately recognise him. I recognise the man who takes my breath away every time I come across him. He's dressed in the same linen I saw him with the other day in Bali, except this time, it's in brown, making his fiery hazel eyes burn with beauty and ambition like never before. He smiles at me when we lock eye contact, and I walk over to him like melting ice.

NICHOLAS

I send Avène a message that I'm in the lobby of her place waiting for her, for as long as she took, it doesn't matter. And after exactly 8 minutes, my love has arrived. Every time I see her, I always think she's growing much more beautiful in my eyes, but this time she blinded my eyes, making me focus on her and only her.

She's wearing a beautiful black dress, making her look surreal. Her eyes in this outfit are drowning me like an Atlantic hurricane. Today, Avène is making me want to blind any man who looks at her, and I'm at service for that.

"Hey, love," I kiss her on the forehead.

"Hey," she blushes.

"Come on, let's head to the surprise I have for you," I take her hand and walk to my car.

Avène remains silent during the ride, listening to the playlist we both decided to put on. This playlist is based on the high school hardships we both went through. It contained moments when we both performed together, moments when we hung out doing fun things, and the time when rumours spread about us, and we had to split for two years. It was the playlist we decided to call *Dawn of Love.*

We reached the location of our first stop on today's date, and Avène finally said something. "No way, we're watching an orchestra?"

"Not any sort of orchestra," I smirk when I see her confusion. "Let's go in, and you'll see."

We take a seat, and as soon as the orchestra starts, Avène realises, "We're the only ones in here, and the song, we performed it before." Her eyes shine under the hall's lights, making me feel weird again. "Did you use one of your tricks again to reserve the entire thing and make them learn it?"

"Yes, love. I used my tricks," I lied. The truth is I've been planning this for years; the orchestra knows these songs by heart by now. I always wanted to show them to Avène, but I never got the chance. After many years, I finally got to show her. The best part is yet to come.

"My love, do you still remember how to play Comptine d'un autre été on the violin?" We sat quietly during the first song, but now it's time to create a core memory.

"Yes, why?" I grab her hand and leave her purse on the chair. We go up the stage, and her eyes shine more than before under the stage lights. "We're performing it?"

"We are," I hand her the violin and go towards the piano. "We aren't just performing; we are creating a moment we will never forget." She smiles, taking a deep breath as I position myself properly.

Avène takes the lead. We have our few seconds of duet before the orchestra joins us, surprising Avène. Although I had planned all this for so long, I never imagined it would be this magical. I look at Avène, who is starting to get emotional but still focuses on the music.

We all play the final note in unison, and after a few moments of silence, Avène starts crying. She cries harder when she locks eye contact with me. It urges me to want to kiss her, but I hold myself back.

It's your first date with her, don't flop it. The back of my mind says, *but their time together is limited,* my heart replies. I've been catching myself talking to myself a lot lately. I must be going insane.

By the time I stopped appreciating Avène's inner and outer beauty, she came over to me and hugged me. I was stunned by how tightly she hugged me and how long she stayed, but I returned the same amount of affection to her to let her know that I cared, whether she was sick or not.

"Proud of you, my love," I whisper to her ear, and I feel her heartbeats increase. "A professional recorded us, by the way, so now we can look back at this moment whenever we want."

She smiles brighter, "Thank you," she replies, "this is the best date I could ask for."

"Oh, there's more to come, sweetheart." I grab her hand. "Come on, we need to go to our next stop." She thanked the orchestra, and we grabbed her purse and left for the next stop of the day.

CHAPTER 25

Avène

We started our date by going to the best orchestra I could've ever asked for, and now we are heading to our next stop. I'm assuming it's a restaurant because I told him I felt hungry, and he said, "Almost there."

What I'm confused about is, if it's a restaurant, why are we entering a place that looks like a palace with guards everywhere, CCTV cameras in every corner, full of only luxury cars, and everything looks like it's made from real gold, pearls, and diamonds.

Glad I came dressed up like this.

"Welcome to Elysium," Nicholas says, confirming my suspicion.

Elysium. A club where only billionaires and millionaires are allowed. That's the only thing the public knows about Elysium; the rest is confidential. "Why are we here?"

"For dinner, of course," he casually says as if he owns the place. I know that Nicholas is a multimillionaire or something, but I never knew he had contact with Elysium.

"Dinner? Do you have a membership here or what?" he laughs when I ask, and my confusion only increases.

"I own the place, sweetheart," I gasp since I don't know how else I can react to this.

He does own the place.

"Since when?" I curiously ask. One thing I don't know about Nicholas is his detailed background. I know that Anderson is his father, and they own PATRICKUS jewels, but I have no idea how, where, when, or why.

"Since ever," he looks at me and starts to explain. "Anderson was the founder of Elysium, just like how he founded PATRICKUS. Now that he's gone, I'm not only a CEO at PATRICKUS and Elysium, but I also own them, which makes me go from a multimillionaire to a billionaire." I feel like I'm watching an American movie again.

"Wow. The baby Nicholas I used to know is such a grown-up billionaire now at the age of twenty-one. Who would have thought?" I say with honest pride.

"I know, right?" he mocks. "People say, 'Don't judge a book by its cover.' You should listen to that advice, my love."

MY LOVE

Two words. Just two words are needed to hold a meaning to the world.

My heart gets flattered whenever I hear it, to the point that my mind mutes all of what he says next and puts "My Love" on repeat. Hearing these two words has been making me want to hold onto life, not caring if it's too late.

The Valet parking takes care of the car, and we head to the room Nicholas reserved, but I ask him to first give me a tour. I mean, it's Elysium? Not everyone can get in. Feels like I'm a main character in a love story.

The exterior had already impressed, but the interior? Wow. Perfection that I cannot describe.

CHAPTER 26
Nicholas

I gave Avène the tour she had asked for, and we dined in a book-themed restaurant I had created for her from scratch. I know that she's been trying to complete her book, so I thought something like this could be an inspiration and romantic.

Once we were done, we walked to the actual library I prepared especially for her in Elysium. The library is decorated with "happy birthday" things since her birthday is tomorrow. She may have thought I forgot, but no, I didn't.

"You remembered," she says. She turns around and looks at me with watery eyes.

"Of course I did," I hug her. "I thought of ways to make this first date special, and this was part of the plan. But what comes up next might either be the worst thing you ever experienced or the best thing."

I kneel and retrieve a box from my pocket. "My love, I know the past few years have been rocky for the both of us, especially lately, but I truly do love you more than anyone else or myself. Will you marry me?" She covers her mouth with her hands, speechless. I give her all the time she needs to answer.

"I would say immediately, yes, with the time limit we have together, and I understand why you would propose so soon, but I feel it's too rushed. Can you ask me again in a week or two?"

"I understand, love." I don't feel hurt or anything. I truly do understand, and it did feel so quick. Even her friends would find it weird. Alex would understand but would find it weird or go into a greater shock. I get up and hold her hand to take her towards the cake, but she stops me.

I turned around, worried why she stopped me, thinking it was one of her symptoms. But she goes cutely on her tiptoes and kisses me quickly. I stare at her with adrenaline rushing through every part of my body and kiss her back harder, not letting her go.

I've been waiting for this to happen for many years now. Sophia was a good kisser, but she wasn't the one for me. Avène is both. She tastes like vanilla, matching the scent of her favourite perfume from Victoria's Secret that she's wearing.

Her lips are so soft that she would make a great candidate to model for Vaseline. "Come on now, I need you to see your cake," she says. She takes my hand with a bright smile on her face, and we go to where I hid the cake.

"Alex!" she says, shocked. "You're able to stand without a wheelchair." She lets go of my hand and goes to hug him and celebrate with him.

"Yes, I'm able! But don't hug me, please, until I put this cake down or you eat it," he warns her at the right time. Avène listens to him, and he puts the cake down and hugs her.

He looks at me when they are done getting so affectionate, and I know right away what he is about to say. I regret inviting him over. "Oh, and can you guys explain to me why you had to kiss so close to where I was standing? The sounds you both made weren't pleasing."

"Why did you have to ruin the mood?" I growl.

"Alex, you always have your ways to embarrass me, don't you?" Avène asks, preparing herself to mess around with him.

"Okay, guys, sorry I asked. Let's cut the cake," he says. He picks up the cake again and sings 'Happy Birthday' to Avène. I would've joined, but singing is not my thing.

We sat down, joking around and talking until midnight, Avène's official birthday, and we brought up our gifts for her. "Should I open Alex's or your gift first?"

"Open his first. You were on your first date with him, not me. It'll make it more special. Trust," Alex suggested when I was going to suggest the opposite.

"Okay then. Let's do this!" Avène says excitedly. We all know she loves unwrapping gifts, so we purposely give them to her every year just for that, no matter how small.

CHAPTER 27

Avène

It's been two weeks since I've had the best 21st birthday ever with the best gifts ever. Nicholas and Alex dropped me back home after I finished unwrapping gifts that I would never have thought I could get from them. Nicholas surprised me with a wedding proposal, which I forced myself to reject, but also a teddy bear from Louis Vuitton that I've been wanting but obviously couldn't afford since it costs at least $2 million. I asked him how he had gotten his hands on it since it had been sold to Jessie Kim, and all he replied was, "I've got my ways." I didn't push him to tell me exactly how since I love plushies, so just owning it is enough for me.

As for Alex, I don't know how he noticed as if he read my bucket list, but he got me a gymnastics leotard, saying I should wear this for my competition programme. Right after that, he announced that he had signed me up for classes. I was going to sign up soon anyway since I have exactly two months left to achieve my entire bucket list now, but Alex made it more meaningful.

Today is my first rehearsal lesson. In the past two weeks, I learned new skills, practised the ones I knew, and got myself ready for a programme my coach and I created together. I chose the song to be "Comptine d'un autre été" as it's the song that holds so many memories for me; it'll match the leotard Alex got me as well.

Other than gymnastics, I've written more on my book, leaving me with two more chapters left. I hung out a lot with Nicholas, too, discovering him in a way I never knew I could ever know about. I also ate Tteokbokki last night with him, which leaves my bucket list looking something like this:

Bucket List:

- *Visit Bali.*
- *Eat Tteokbokki.*
- *Compete in gymnastics.*
- *Become a sports journalist*
- *Spend fun time with Alex.*
- *Gossip more with girls.*
- *Never see Nicholas again.*

I know that there are two things I won't definitely achieve on this bucket list. One is becoming a sports journalist, and two is never seeing Nicholas again. Bali is a point that I won't be able to cross out. It all became so clear to me in the past few weeks. I've been hanging out with the girls every weekend, eating Tteokbokki yesterday, starting to prepare for my gymnastics competition, having fun with Alex every day, and seeing Nicholas every other day. All this, despite my symptoms that have been worsening, and I almost got caught in front of the girls.

I've accepted that the things that aren't meant to be crossed out won't get crossed out, no matter how hard I fight with life. It is still upsetting that I won't be shown as a great sports journalist on TV, but hopefully, by publishing my book soon, I can be remembered.

I go down to Alex, who's been waiting for me at the reception for the past 10 minutes and is about to go crazy. He has been dropping me off for my classes ever since I started, and I love it. It brings back memories of when he would go to the ice rink with me and support me, although he can't even glide.

"Bro, just explain this to me," he says, examining my outfit. "Why do girls always take ages to get ready, although their outfit is as basic as yours?" I look at him and start to judge him.

Basic? How is my outfit basic? I'm wearing Lululemon leggings with a crop top and leg warmers, can't see how that's basic. "Then you explain this for me." I got closer to his face to scare him with my eye contact. "Why do guys have no fashion sense?"

"Get in the car," he says, mad that he can't reply to that one. Or if he does, I'll continue to roast him. I gestured a peace sign to him before I continued to walk to the car.

The entire car ride, we blasted Deadpool and Wolverine's soundtrack like kids because that movie was a banger. Period. By the time we reached my institute, Alex had memorised the *Bye Bye Bye* dance and was planning to perform it for my coach. I was proud but wanted to disappear from embarrassment.

I finished my lesson peacefully after convincing Alex not to show him and giving him an entire pros and cons lecture on why it would be so bad if he showed him. I changed my outfit to something more classic, which Alex gave me to change into, saying we were going somewhere but not giving me a clue where. Unusual for him to keep a surprise.

Shockingly, we changed the Deadpool soundtrack to Frozen. Alex said I had to be as womanly as possible before we reached wherever we were going.

CHAPTER 28
Nicholas

"Alex, I want to marry Avène," I announce the minute Alex and I sit and get our drinks. The last time I confessed to Avène, Alex didn't know I would propose, but he did know we had been madly in love since the first day I ever saw her.

The last time I confessed, it went wrong. Either way, but this time, I want to do it right. I'm not doing it out of pity, just because she's dying soon. I'm doing it because I want to be part of her final moments. I want to have meaning in her life, like she has in mine.

I don't need to get permission from Alex since it's Avène and my life, but Alex is like a brother to me. I wouldn't want to put him in another shock. "Are you serious?" he finally asks after a stretched silence.

"Dead serious," I answer with no hesitation.

"Then propose," his expression changes into one I don't recognise. "I trust you. After all you've done, I trust you to be the one with Avène until her last breath." I get the weird feeling that I tried to recognise what it is so many times but failed to do so.

"Thank you." I genuinely do feel grateful for him. I always get what I want either way, but whatever Alex does for me, I always feel thankful. "I want to propose tonight. Can you help me with it?"

"Of course, I'll be your assistant who makes sure everything is perfect," he smiles at me and taps my shoulder.

God, it is so thrilling not to tell Raven about it. "She has gymnastics today, right?" he nods a yes. "Why don't I send you the location of the place I want to set up, and you bring her there, saying there's somewhere she needs to go before going home."

"Sounds like a plan," he stays silent for a bit, and he gets an idea to add to this plan. "How about we go buy something fancy for her right now to wear? I know her style, and I'm sure she won't pack a change of clothes that isn't athletic with her." This is another pro of discussing the proposal with Alex; siblings do come in handy.

"Finish your drink, and let's go before you need to pick her up." We finish our drinks and go to the nearest mall. Alex immediately goes into a store I've never heard of, but it's called Bershka and says that it's Avène's favourite.

Thanks to Alex making everything easier, he found a cute fancy sky blue set that I also agree would match Avène perfectly. I pay for it, and Alex and I part ways. He goes to pick up Avène, and I go make sure everything is perfect.

Everything is now ready, and I see Alex parking his car. I feel much more nervous compared to last time. A couple of minutes after that, I see Avène and Alex getting out of the car. Avène does have sharp eyes, so she notices me from afar. Far away, she was already looking miraculous, but with every step she came near, she looked fabulous.

Her beauty is also the reason I feel nervous. If she says yes, I get to see her breathtaking ocean eyes every single day, and I wouldn't want something more than that. "Nicholas, what's going on?" she asks when she reaches where I'm standing.

"I have a surprise for you, my love," I take her hand, and we walk towards the table I set up on the beach decorated with all her favourite flowers, making sure it meets her expectations. It was simple enough to plan a setup for the proposal since ever since we were teenagers, she would always live in delusions where her future man confesses to her in a beach setup, and today, I'm going to make her delusions real.

We reach, and I already see her face doing a wow expression, which gets a chuckle out of me. "What? Did you just laugh?" she asks, as if she'll kill me if I deny or be honest.

"It's just cute how you're admiring it all, makes me feel a weird feeling," I look into her shining eyes and tell myself that this was the perfect moment. "That being said..." I hold her hand. "I'm nervous. I know, so unusual, but excuse any mistakes." She nods with a bright smile, listening without saying a word.

"My Love,
I never fell for blue eyes,
Until you gave me butterflies.
Every time I rise,
I drown in your eyes.
That's when I realised,
I can fall for your eyes.
In a world where I'm filled with darkness,
You are my brightness.
In a world where I'm empty,
You are my plenty.
My lead, my chant, my dove.
I need you, want you, love you,"

"Will you marry me?" I kneel and retrieve the ring from my pocket.

My chest was heaving, waiting to hear her answer. I had never planned to confess using a poem I wrote for her when I missed her.

"Yes!" I stay looking at her, stunned, forgetting to be a gentleman and putting the ring on her. If there's one person who will make me lose my mind and act like a kid, it's Avène.

She already got emotional the minute I started speaking, but now I started crying before her. I got up and hugged her so she didn't see my crying face for long. It's embarrassing too. The last time I cried was when my mother passed away. "It's fine, you can show me your crying face. I won't judge you; we need to normalise men crying, anyways," she says as if she heard the conversation I just had with my brain.

"Not now; let me hug you for one more minute," I beg.

"Okay," she tightens her hug, showing her appreciation through it. "Thank you for the poem you worked so hard on. I didn't know I needed to hear anything like that until I did."

"I know. I didn't know I needed to say it too," I break the hug and start acting the way I'm supposed to. "Okay, Ms Avène Valikova. Please do give me your hand." I formally ask to put the ring on, hoping the size is correct.

It ended up being the right size, and I couldn't feel any happier. "You're mine now, love." I take her mouth like a starved wild animal. Her vanilla scent and taste are something I'll never not want as an appetiser.

Can't wait to tell Raven about my life changes.

CHAPTER 29
Avène

Eleven hours ago, I had the proposal I never would have imagined I could get. The setup, the atmosphere, the dinner, and Nicholas's poem especially. His poem repaired and broke my heart. I wished we were a normal couple with at least five years of lifetime left.

His cries were definitely mixed with happiness and sorrow. All these seven years we spent together, I never once saw Nicholas cry until yesterday. I hope my loved ones, like him, don't shed those tears at my funeral.

We planned to keep our engagement a secret as it would be so bizarre for everyone to understand unless we told them the truth about my health. We won't announce anything until the day I compete in gymnastics, which is July 30th, and we're planning to marry on August 5th. I'll have around ten days with Nicholas left after marriage, but at least we are engaged now, and he can call me his, and I can call him mine.

I have exactly a week until the competition, and my symptoms have been worsening, but I'm trying to maintain them until I am, at least in my final month, done with my goals. I truly don't want to become paralysed or unable to speak before then. I still haven't thanked Anastasia yet for all these years and for being my soon-to-be maid of honour.

What scared me the most was when Alex handed me the outfit I had to wear before going to Nicholas. I didn't remember who he was for a few seconds. The one person I surely don't want to forget about is Alex. He's been with me in every step of my life, even more than my parents or any other human being in this world. I want to remember him in my next life as well.

I just came back from gymnastics rehearsal, and since I miss Anastasia, I called her to see what her plans are. "What's up, girl?" she replies immediately.

"Were you watching Instagram reels again?" I ask because every time she replies this fast, she's either on TikTok or Instagram reels.

"Yes, why?" I knew it.

"Nothing, I just knew it," I do a little celebratory dance for being right. "Anyways, got plans for today?"

"I'm free if you exclude my psychology homework," I know that she's messing around since it's summer vacation.

"You're messing around. It's summer, bro?" she chuckles when she knows she can't trick me. We go to the same university.

"Yeah, but I'm free. What do you wanna do?" She sounds amused to spend the day with me.

"Let's go to the cinema. I wanna rewatch Deadpool." I have a Deadpool hoodie that I wore to every single Deadpool movie, and now I'm going to use it to rewatch Deadpool.

"Yesssss, I love Deadpool!" she exclaimed. "Do I pick you up, or do you?"

"I'll borrow Alex's car and come over to you." I do have my driving licence, but I just don't like using it unless it's for a hangout like this. "I'll be there in an hour."

"Okay, see you, hottie."

"See ya, cutie." I hung up and called Alex to let me borrow the car. He did tell me earlier that he has no plans, so he should be okay with giving it to me.

"Alex, I need you to do me a favour, please," I say when he answers.

"Bring it on," he sounds like he's in a good mood.

"Can you please let me borrow your car?" I straightforwardly request. "I want to go with Anastasia to watch Deadpool, so I won't be alone. Don't worry."

He stays silent for a few moments, hesitating, but he eventually agrees, "Fine, but you better be safe."

"I will." I was about to hang up, but then I got the urge to thank him for whatever reason. "Alex, thank you for everything."

"Welcome? That was random," he says worriedly. "Are you okay?"

"Yes, I am. I just realised I never thanked you, so I wanted to say it," I say honestly.

"Okay, thank you also for everything," he chuckles. "Now, go get ready before I bring the car to you." We both hang up, and I go get ready.

CHAPTER 30
Avène

I give Alex our traditional hug when he brings the car to my place, and I head out to pick up Anastasia. "Ana, I'll be there in ten minutes, on my way," I send her a voice message, to which she replies with a thumbs up.

I start the car ride by blasting the Deadpool one playlist and singing along with it with all my heart. I haven't ridden a car alone in a while, and this feels so good to experience. Living the dream by having a karaoke session in the car on my way to my best friend.

After some time, Google Maps showed me that I had five minutes left to reach my destination, but I didn't remember where I was going or how I was in the car. I try to remember by looking at the address and going through my messages on my phone, but it doesn't work. I only get more confused. How is it July already?

I keep on looking through my phone, the pictures, and chats, and I find out that I've been chatting with someone named Ana. I do send her a message to remind me who she is, but my message doesn't get sent as my data finishes. I keep on going in circles on the same road, confused as to where I am and how I got here because I don't remember ever owning a car.

I decided to just keep on driving anywhere but the location on Google Maps. Who knows what could be waiting for me at that location? I kept on going forward, praying to God to show me the right path and let me remember how I got into this car. I started to feel the panic hitting me when I couldn't remember a single thing, no matter how hard I tried for more than ten minutes.

The panic started to take over me until I started to hear the playlist and my phone ringing, muffled and unable to see where it was or where I was going. "Breathe, Avène, breathe," I hear a honk from afar, making me panic even more.

"One tap, two taps, three." If only Alex or Nicholas were here to help me out. I realise that my memories are coming back, or at least I'm starting to remember people who played a huge role in my life. The realisation helped me calm down and gradually return my eyesight to normal, but it was too late for that.

My life ends here. I'll end up being killed by a truck, not my illness. It makes me feel better since no one will see me paralysed or forgetful, but dying alone right now doesn't feel so good. I'm terrified. I didn't say what I wanted to say to anyone except for Alex.

I haven't achieved my goals yet. My book is incomplete. I didn't perform my gymnastics routine yet. I didn't get married to my dawn of love or tell him that I love him. For my brother, no one knows what exact hospital he's in. Does that mean he'll die today with me?

I feel my consciousness fading away as people crowd around me after getting me out of the car. What an unfair life.

CHAPTER 31
Nicholas

Alex and I meet up after he drops off his car at Avène's. We go to the bar, sit to joke around, discuss some things, and play a few games where the loser must drink shots. We keep on going at it until I receive a call from Avène.

"Who's calling you?" drunk Alex asks. He's now on his tenth shot after ten losses in a total of twelve rounds. I lost twice.

"Avène," I say, preparing to hear her voice, which will make me want to see her right away.

"Oh, she is supposed to be with Anastasia, but I guess she misses you," Alex continues to fantasise about Avène and me, but I ignore him and answer the call so as not to keep her waiting.

"Hey, love," I pick up the call.

"Is this Mr Nicholas?" an unknown voice picks up the call, and I become concerned.

"Yes, who's this?" I furiously ask.

"A nurse from Massachusetts General Hospital," she states, and I start to think of all the scenarios as to why a hospital would call me on Avène's phone.

"A nurse?" I feel my blood boiling. "Why would you call me on my girlfriend's phone?" I growl.

"Mr. Nicholas, I'm sorry to announce, but your girlfriend got into an accident earlier," she takes a deep breath. "Please come to the hospital to fill out some paperwork, and we can explain to you how the accident happened."

"How's her condition?" I ask, making Alex get up and follow me.

"We can discuss it when you come." She's been limiting all the details, and my worry has only been growing.

I don't explain to Alex what's going on or why we are rushing to the hospital out of nowhere since he's drunk and still fantasising about me and Avène.

We reach the hospital, and I rush to the emergency reception. "I received a phone call twenty minutes ago from one of your nurses about patient Avène Valikova. Can I know where I can talk to the doctors or where I can see Avène?"

"Yes, it was me who called you," she says, staring at Alex. "Is the gentleman behind you alright?"

I look back at Alex, and from his facial expression, I know he will vomit soon. "He got a bit drunk after so many drinks. Can one of the nurses help him out? He'll vomit soon," I state, and he starts to gag.

"Yes, they'll take care of him." A male nurse comes and takes Alex wherever. I'll check on him after I know where Avène is and why they aren't telling me enough information about her.

"Thank you. Can I know more about Avène?" I ask, getting impatient.

"Mr. Nicholas, do you know that Avène has been suffering from Glioblastoma?" she starts.

"Yes, and she has two months left now," I answer.

"Her symptoms have been worsening lately, and today especially, she experienced memory loss, forgetting where she was supposed to go and couldn't recall her friends, including you. This led her to panic, resulting in severe panic attacks." Forget that illness and those panic attacks. "Ms Avène couldn't see where she was going, so even when she heard the truck honking, she couldn't get away from it, leading to an accident."

"Avène has been suffering from panic attacks for seven years. They stopped, but a month ago, she randomly started getting them again. How's her condition now?" she looks up at me, looking sorrowful.

"I'm sorry when we reached there, it was too late," she takes a deep breath and announces, "Ms Avène passed away at 6:04 PM."

"Sorry?" is the only word that could come out of my mouth.

"We tried everything we could to reach there as fast as we could, but it was too late," she repeats.

"Then what's the damn point of having 911 services?" I snapped at her when I couldn't digest the information she fed me.

"I'm sorry," she apologises as if an apology will bring back the dead.

"There's a video that I'm assuming Ms. Avène recorded before the accident occurred. It helped us figure out the details of the accident, but I think there's something that'll help you accept things." She hands me Avène's phone.

"What room is the guy that was with me earlier in?" I ask, looking down at Avène's phone, which I'm holding.

"221," the same room Avène was admitted to when her panic attacks came back. "Please, when you feel a bit better, do come so we can fill out paperwork and plan for the funeral." I nod and go to Alex.

I reached Alex's room, where they gave him some medication to stop the vomiting and improve his hangover. I find him asleep, so I sit next to him, speechless and staring at Avène's phone, trying to understand and accept all this.

For the first time since my mother's death, I couldn't think straight. It all happened so fast. What would I tell Alex? She was my first love, but she was Alex's sister. What would I tell Anastasia, who's still waiting for Avène to pick her up? She's called Avène ten times.

Alex and I thought we had more time to prepare and tell others about Avène's illness, but now she has died. She suffered three times more: Glioblastoma, panic attacks, and a car accident. What an unfair life.

I continued to stare at the dark screen on the phone in the silent room until Alex woke up. "Nicholas?"

"Oh, Alex, you're up," I tap on his shoulder absent-mindedly.

"What's wrong, and why am I here even though I was just drunk?" he asks, looking like he is back to his normal self.

"This will be hard to understand, but you need to listen," I say, giving myself some time to say it out loud to him.

"Did something bad happen again?" he asks, and I wish it was just something 'bad.'

"Yeah," he started to look concerned, and I started explaining to him, "Do you remember the call I got in the bar that was supposed to be Avène?"

"Partially, yes," he tries to remember more but isn't able to.

"That call wasn't Avène. It was the nurse from this hospital," I break it down to him step by step as I worry he faces something greater than paralysis this time.

"Why? Did she get another symptom?" Alex didn't overthink the other, worse scenario.

"Partially, yes, but something else happened." I can't say it out loud or make eye contact with him. It feels clogged in my throat.

"What is it, Nicholie? You can tell me," he holds my hand, which is unusual for him, as if he already knows where this conversation is going.

I kept on hesitating, but I eventually made my way there. "Her symptom was forgetfulness. She forgot she was going to meet Anastasia, or that you're Alex, or that I'm Nicholas. She forgot it was your car she's driving."

"And?" he encourages me to continue.

"That led her to panic. She panicked to the point she couldn't see where she was driving," I state.

"So, she got into an accident?" he asks, making his voice even gentler.

"Yeah," I need to carry on and tell him exactly what accident she got into, but the clogging feeling comes back.

"How's her condition now?" he asks, the same question I had asked the nurse earlier.

"Alex, a truck hit her," I announce.

"Yeah, I get it, but how's her condition?" he repeats himself, the same way I did earlier.

I stay silent, trying to push through the clog, but it doesn't work. I can't say it out loud. It'll be real, then. I can't say it out loud. "Nicholas, whatever is going on, you must tell me what it is," he takes a deep breath. "I can handle it, trust me."

I look down at Avène's phone and whisper, "6:04 PM. Avène passed away." I look up at him. "She's dead." His facial expression changed so fast; I knew what he was thinking.

"It's not your fault just because you let her borrow your car, so don't blame yourself." His hands started to feel cold compared to when he first held me.

Unlike me, Alex knows how to cry when things are hard, and I'm proud of him for crying immediately instead of keeping it in. I get up from my chair and hug him. I'm not that affectionate, but in times like these, I would give all the affection I have left for Alex. "You have the right to show your emotions too, Nicholas.

Don't keep it in," he whispers in my ear when I hug him.

I do feel the clog in my throat, but there isn't a single tear coming out. "I'm fine."

"Liar," he says. "But where's Avène now?" He seems to be accepting this faster than I am.

"You're accepting this?" It feels so weird to know he is accepting this so fast after seeing him not being able to accept her illness.

"Yeah, ever since we found out she was dying, I've been preparing myself. I just didn't know she would be taken away this fast." Life throws at us things we never expect, and it shocks us for a while, but I've never seen someone like Nicholas accept everything so fast. I don't trust him, so I will keep a close eye on him.

"Whatever you say... but no, I don't know where she is. When they told me, I was too stunned to ask for any more information. I didn't even call Anastasia back; she must be going crazy right now," I justify. "Any ideas on how to tell her?"

"Yeah, call her from Avène's phone, and I'll talk to her." I give him Avène's phone, and that's when I see the blood stain on the case. I have no idea what that triggered, but I started randomly crying like a little boy who was lost.

While I was confused as to why I was randomly crying, Alex understood and hugged me, reciprocating the affection that I had given him. We stayed like that for a few moments until I calmed down enough for him to call Anastasia.

She immediately picks up and shoots questions: "I've called thirty-five times, sent you messages, reels, and TikTok videos to get your attention, but you never answered. What happened? How did it happen, and what is going on?"

Alex takes a deep breath before answering her so he doesn't break down while he explains. "Ana, it's me, Alex."

"Why isn't Avène answering me?" Avène has earned herself a true friend.

"I'll explain now if you allow me," she finally stays silent as Alex explains and then announces, "They weren't able to save her. She's dead."

Anastasia stays silent, and the more I look at that blood stain on the phone with the silence, the more all this feels so real. I can't accept it. I feel another clog of tears is about to break out, so I leave the room without telling Alex where I'm going.

I wash my face after having another crying session alone in the bathroom and head back to Alex. I don't trust him enough to leave him alone in that room.

I reached his room when I heard loud sobs coming from it, and that's when I was sure he didn't accept it.

I let him let it out without knowing I was there at the door, patiently waiting for him to calm down. I waited for ten minutes until I started hearing something in his room opening and hearing so many strange sounds coming from it. I quickly open the door and see him holding onto the window.

"Alex, no," I gently say as I stand slightly close to him, afraid one more step will make him do it. "Alex, we can overcome this together, please." Losing both of the closest people I fought so hard for wouldn't just make me act like a lost boy; it'll make me kill myself with them.

"I can't live without her, Nicholas. This will put my pain to ease," he says, crying. "Thank you for everything. I'll forever remember you." He smiled, and as he was about to jump off, I ran, closing the distance between us before it was too late.

I caught his hand as he hung on the wall, gradually pulling him back up. It was hard to the point I thought my hand might get slippery and he'd fall and lose him, but I did it.

I hug him tighter than ever to show him how much I need him. "Don't ever do that again," I say, locking eye contact with him. "I know how hard it is. I've also lost my mother and now Avène. I know it's hard, but if we listen and help each other, we can overcome it. Not by moving on, but by getting stronger."

I don't know if I'm doing something wrong as it's my first time having to comfort someone when their close one died, but he goes back up to that window and tries to do it again until I push him back for the second time.

"Alex, please don't," my voice starts to crack. "I swear you're all I have left." He doesn't listen to me and gets up again, but this time, he doesn't go to the window since he knows I'll stop him. He runs out into the corridor towards the nurse station.

I got up and ran after him. When I reached him, I found him barging into the nurse's station and picking up the sharpest thing he could find near him. It was too late for me to stop him; he stabbed himself. But when he wanted to stab himself the second time, I came in perfect time, stopping him. I got hurt with him, but hopefully, this gets him to wake up at least a bit.

It's like he lost his mind within a second. I remove the scalpel from his hands and go to the nurses to tell them to treat him. Unfortunately, they all got worried when he barged in and ran off somewhere, so I had to look for them while I was losing blood.

I found the emergency reception, and the nurse had broken the news to me. I explained the situation to her and showed her where Alex was. They took him to get surgery since he stabbed himself deeply in the intestine. I waited there, standing still, losing more blood as I refused treatment and insisted on waiting here until I saw him awake and doing okay.

I tried my best to retain my consciousness, but I started to feel dizzy and warm. I collapsed.

CHAPTER 32
Nicholas

I wake up to find myself sleeping in a hospital bed with an IV in my hand. For a second, I don't remember what happened until the pain kicks in, and I realise what a day it has been. A nurse comes in and explains to me that I've had an operation on my hand, had fifty-two stitches, and that I should now wait until the IV gives me back all the blood I had lost. I ignore them, remove the IV even though my hand is dripping blood again, and go find Alex.

I can't leave him alone. What if he wakes up and thinks about committing suicide again? I stopped by a receptionist and asked them briefly about how to get someone admitted to the psychiatric ward. After seeing that earlier, Alex surely needs to get admitted until he calms down and understands that even if our dearest passes away, we need to fight through for them and continue to live.

She gave me the details and informed me which room Alex was in. I go to him and find him still unconscious. In the meantime, I return to my room to get my phone and then go back to Alex. However, the nurse stops me and repeats herself, emphasising the importance of finishing my IV and stopping the bleeding. I ignore her and proceed back to Alex. What she's saying is right, but I can't sacrifice Alex just for me to relax.

I sit in the quiet room and start setting up arrangements for Alex to get admitted to the psychiatric ward. He won't accept it and might hate me for it, but I'd rather that than him dying. I click on 'done' and sit staring at the floor, waiting for him to wake, but then I remember Avène's phone.

The nurse said there's a recording there that I must see, so I go towards the nightstand that's next to Alex's bed and I pick up her phone. I try my best to not look at Avène's blood stain, so I don't get triggered as last time, and I continue to guess her password.

After getting her phone blocked six times and trying to guess twenty-eight times, it worked, and it made me feel even more guilty.

"170622" June 17, 2022, the day when she had her fourteenth birthday, three days after, it was chaos. My eyes were fixed on Avène ever since the first day she joined our school, but her early birthday party happened too soon. We haven't gotten to connect enough, yet she invited me. Her friends knew that she liked me, and they all acted neutral about it. That day, we indeed had a blast, but it all shattered.

Avène used to be very gullible. She would believe the lies her friends and I had told to the extent that her closest friend snitched to me that she liked me. I knew that she did, but I couldn't like her back. I had no power to protect the love of my life when I was a teenager, and God, I treated her awfully when those rumours spread. I argued with her and ignored her even when she sat in front of me in classes, and there were times when I got worried about her, making her even more confused for an entire year.

I decided to apologise when I saw her charm never broke, even with the people who hurt her the most. I knew at that moment that I'd never get enough of her. She forgave, and we became neutral friends, but there were times when we would cut contact for months. It continued like that until lately; now she's gone. My goal was to sincerely apologise to her on our wedding day. That day will never come now.

I ignore the guilt until I at least see the recording before Alex wakes up and hears it. There were crashing sounds almost the entire time, but then I started to hear Avène talk in pain. "I don't know if it's recording, but if you see this, then I'm dead. I couldn't say this to any of you guys but thank you for everything. I wish I could specify more, but as you can hear, there isn't enough time." She coughs, and after a while, she continues. "This all happened so fast. I'm sorry to disappoint you all. I kept my illness hidden so you don't get hurt. Please don't cry at my funeral; smile and laugh at all the jokes I made in the past." She stayed silent for a while till I almost thought that was her last breath. "Nicholas, I forgave you long ago, and it was never your fault. I'm sorry I argued back. I've always loved and still do. Don't blame this on you." She takes a deep breath. "Alex, this isn't your fault. Buy yourself a new car with the money I left for you, please. Don't repair this one. I love you, and fix your attitude for your future wife." She sounds like she is coughing blood or something and continues to deliver the message. "Anastasia, I'm sorry for not watching Deadpool with you. Learn the dance and perform it for me at my funeral, and I'll dance back." What she said next is what made me start crying again. "Please don't forget me, guys. Talk about me at least once a year. I'm scared enough to be dying alone now. I love yo-"

I hear many people crowding around her and screaming to get some help. Someone later picks up Avène's phone, which is still recording, and I get a glimpse of her. It breaks my heart. She took all those injuries by herself. Alex and I should never have allowed her to drive the car alone.

An hour passed, and Alex finally woke up. "Alex, how do you feel?"

He stays quiet, looking around, and takes a long time to answer. "It didn't work." He looks at me. "Why the fuck did it not work, Nicholas?"

"*Fuck?*" he swore. For the first time in our ten years of friendship, this is how I confirm that Alex needs to stay at the psychiatric ward for some time.

"Because you're meant to stay in this life and be with me," I say, hiding my worry. "I need a drinking buddy; otherwise, I'll be all alone. You know how bad I am at making friends," I joke to lighten up his mood.

"Forget this life," he swears again. "I'll try my best not to let this life win." He tries to get up but collapses, thanks to the anaesthesia.

I help him go back to his bed, and he grabs my hand, which is still dripping blood, examining it. "It's nothing, don't worry."

"Did I do this to you?" he asks.

"You don't remember?" I answer out of pure concern, not overthinking what this could trigger for him.

"See, this further proves that I shouldn't exist in this life anymore." Shit.

"That's booger bullshit because you should and deserve to still exist. I need you, Alex, open your fucking eyes, bro," I snap at him. "If I didn't need you, I wouldn't even sit here caring for you or put my life in danger."

I helped him back to his bed and let him rest since he calmed down a bit more, thankfully. He won't be moved to the psych ward until tomorrow, so I must stay awake for his sake or ask a nurse to give him medication to calm him.

I made sure that he was asleep before I went to the nurse's reception. I explained to them his condition, and that he'll be moved to the psych ward tomorrow, so he just needs some sedatives to sleep through the night. They agreed, and another nurse raised my concern again.

I am starting to feel slightly lightheaded, so I accept the offer of them stopping the bleeding and IV, but I accept it with the condition of doing it in Alex's room.

CHAPTER 33
Nicholas

Two days ago, Avène passed away. Alex lost it, and Anastasia, no one has heard from her. These two days have been full of me visiting Alex whenever I'm free. The rest of the time, I am either filling out paperwork, preparing for Avène's funeral, checking on my office, or sitting in the fields at night talking to the stars, pretending it to be Avène.

Cassie has been handling all my workload ever since I told her my fiancée had passed away, so I'm thankful for her. I've started to accept Avène's death not because I don't love her but because I don't want to burden her and want to be strong for Alex and her friends, who have no idea that she passed away, other than Anastasia.

Today, the plans are to go and talk to Alex's psychiatrist, as they called me requesting to have a conversation with me. I'll then visit him and go check on Anastasia. If Anastasia is doing well, I want to break the news to the rest of Avène's friends since the funeral will be held tomorrow.

Until now, I haven't seen Avène's corpse. I've been hesitating endlessly as I accept the fact that she's gone, but I can't get it into my head yet that I'll never see her anymore. I'll force myself to make the decision tonight as it'll be my last chance, given this opportunity.

I reach the psych ward where Alex is staying and enter a room where I find his psychiatrist waiting for me alongside his nurse. "Hello, Mr Nicholas. Please have a seat," she greets me.

I take the seat and greet her back, "Hello, Ms. Hannah. How's Alex getting along with all of you?"

"He's been improving quite a lot since yesterday, especially after we found the perfect antidepressants for him. They have been helping him accept the fact that his family friend has passed away. He's a lovely boy, caring for other patients all the time," she smiles.

"Yes, he's always been caring in our friend group as well," I smile like a proud older brother. "Since he's improving, when can he get discharged?"

"Yes, that's what I wanted to discuss with you. He could be discharged tomorrow and go to the surgery treatment ward since his wound from the injury hasn't healed yet. He could also generally get discharged and heal it at home, but I'm concerned about the environment there and about your health as well; you've been looking unwell these days." She looks at my injured hand.

"The environment at my house is normal, and that's where I'm going to let him stay. We are holding Avène's funeral tomorrow, but if it's risky for him to attend, then I'll keep him at home without knowing I'm at the funeral, with supervision, of course." I've already thought about this scenario, so I answer her without hesitation. "And you don't have to be concerned about my health; my injury is from when I stopped Alex from injuring himself, and my eye bags are because I've been busy with preparations and letting others know." I lie; the reason behind my eye bags is that I can't sleep at all; the sight of Avène in the recorded video has been replayed every night.

"I would suggest he attends the funeral. His not attending will confuse him as to whether all this is real or not, which could cause a delay in his acceptance. However, please do know that there might be an attack triggered by being in that environment." I started to get concerned after hearing her say that, but I didn't show it. "A way to maintain this is by carrying the medication with you."

"Okay, no worries, I can deal with it," I agree, and we continue to talk about how long Alex should take his medication, the process, and the quantity.

After the meeting, Alex's nurse took me to see him and inform him of the good news. I sit with him, and I can already sense that the Alex I know is coming back. "What's up, man?" I casually start the conversation.

"Nothing much. I miss home," he says straightforwardly.

"I've got good news," I smile. "You're coming home with me tomorrow!" he brightens up and finally locks eye contact with me.

"Fun," he smiles and stops almost immediately. "What about Avène's funeral? Did it already take place?"

"No, it'll happen tomorrow, and you will be there with me. Is that okay?"

"Yeah." He stays silent for a moment but eventually gets the courage to ask, "What about Ana? Did you reach her?"

"I'm planning to go see her today. I need to also inform her other friends. I don't think Anastasia told them yet," I look into his eyes and ask, "Alex."

"Yeah?"

"Remember Avène's brother, Denis?" She hasn't mentioned him in the video, so I'm concerned about where he might be.

"Yeah?"

"Do you know where he is or what he's up to?" Alex is the closest to Avène, so she should tell him at least.

"Nope. She hardly ever talks about him," he takes a deep breath. "I don't know if she told you this before, but back when we were younger, he and I were so close. He's a good guy, even with his mental illnesses, but Avène hated him while he loved her." I never knew this; all I knew was he had autism and other difficulties and was older than her. "At first, he only had thoughts like a child, so he had a delay in education. But as we grew up, at the age of 9, he started getting tantrums. The worst one I ever experienced was when we were fifteen. That's when Avène stopped talking about him in general, and that's when she developed some mental illnesses, including panic attacks."

"I never knew this," the guilty feeling comes back. If only I had known all this, I would've treated her better, but at the same time, she might not have liked it since it would have been out of pity. But I honestly do feel horrible; I only added more pain to her life.

"Yeah, it's something only I know," he smiles. "Avène had a tough life and died unfairly. Her actual dream all these years was to be married and have kids so she could feel what an ordinary life truly feels like. But all that isn't your fault, including her panic attacks; they didn't happen because of you." He taps on my shoulder. "She loved you and still does; remember her that way."

This is something no one knew, but every time I looked at Avène, she shined like a star, filling the sky beautifully. That's why now, every night, I talk to the stars, imagining it's her. My love will forever be my first and last.

"I'll remember her like that," I finally reply. The other two people are concerning me, and since we are talking about Avène's life, I might as well bring them up, especially since he looks calm in answering my questions. "So, you don't know where Denis is?"

"Nope," he shakes his head.

"What about her parents?" His facial expression changed immediately.

"Nicholas, you know why I couldn't accept Avène was dead before I came here?" he breaks eye contact with me.

"No? Tell me if you feel like it." I'm afraid of forcing conversations on him yet since he just started to stabilise.

"They passed away last year. Avène last spoke with them during Christmas when they hung up the phone on her just because Avène raised her voice a bit. They were drunk and got into an accident, just like Avène; they got hit by a truck." He sighs. "My parents are the ones who informed me about their death, and you know what's worse? They wrote their entire will for their dog; they left millions for a dog, leaving nothing for their son or daughter. Avène never found out about their death because I never told her, neither did my parents, and no one called Avène as their guardian because her parents deleted her phone number that night." The guilt increases the more I know about the life Avène lived.

"I never knew her parents were this bad." I'm honestly shocked. Such an awful thing to do to your daughter. I thought I had a bad life, but at least I experienced true parental love from my mother. It was a short duration, but I experienced it, unlike Avène, who had never done it.

"Yeah, I know. That's why I felt guilty and couldn't accept a word that came out of your mouth that night. She even died in the same scenario as her parents, just with a different reason behind it. She died without saying goodbye to any of us, especially her brother, or knowing her parents had passed away a year ago. I felt like I failed to be the brother she needed."

I hugged him as his words made me feel weird again. I think long about it, but I feel I want to let him listen to Avène's final recording without letting him know how she looks at the end of the video. I feel like it could strengthen him more. If it works with him, it should work with Anastasia and her other friends, too. "Alex, I want to show you something before I get going."

I show him the video. When he hears the part where she gives the message to him, he starts crying but smiling. "Thank you for showing this to me, it feels comforting."

"I'm glad," I get up and head towards the exit.

"Thank you for everything. I consider you as the brother I've been wanting for a long time," he says happily.

"You can count on me anytime." I leave and head to Anastasia's place, based on the location Avène shared with me a long time ago, to pick her up.

I reached Anastasia's house and was shocked when Evelyn opened the door to let me in. I found Avène's entire friend group there. One was crying, another was sobbing, another swore, and another told the story of how she died.

"Hello, ladies. I'm sorry to interrupt, but I came to check on you all since Anastasia hasn't been replying." I scan the room to find Anastasia, but she is nowhere to be found.

"I would crush on you if only it wasn't my best friend that died because you're a hottie," Isabella mutters. She looks at me the same way those nurses were at the hospital. I just didn't have the energy to ask them why they were idolising me through their stares, but Isabella made it clear.

"Shut up," Charlotte and Eleanor say in unison.

Eleanor comes up to me and finally answers the reason why I'm here. "We only found out about Avène today when we tried calling her and Ana to hang out with us. None of them answered, so when Eve came to check on Ana since they live close by, Ana opened the door for her but later collapsed." She starts crying but pushes through, "I called my personalised doctor for her when Eve called me panicking, and he said she collapsed because ever since the day Alex broke the news to her, she hasn't eaten or drunk enough water and didn't see any sunlight. She's now resting in her room."

"Okay, please do take care of her. I'll let you guys accept the fact that Avène is gone now, but I just want you to know tomorrow the funeral will be held. Do come if you're able. Let Anastasia come as well, even in a wheelchair. It'll help her. I'm forcing Alex to come."

"Okay, but how did Avène even die? And what happened to Alex? Ana didn't tell us anything; she didn't wake up yet." I take a seat to explain everything from A to Z, and once I do, I let them grieve together as I'm sure they have each other's backs and continue with the things I must do today.

I called Cassie earlier, telling her to find Avène's brother no matter what in an hour. To her credit, she did achieve it. I went there to see his condition and understand more about him since I've decided to take responsibility for him from now on.

I've asked the hospital to let me take him out for the funeral tomorrow. They agreed, but said it must be done with a nurse accompanying him. This arrangement was great since I must stay focused with Alex.

After finishing that, I decided to go and see Avène's corpse. Even if it will haunt me or have a severe side effect on me, after hearing Alex tell me about her life, I couldn't let her be buried without anyone checking on her beforehand.

It takes me only a few seconds to look at her before I feel that feeling again and start crying. The number of tears I cried over Avène is more than with my mother. I'm glad I took days off from work; otherwise, the employees are going to make a whole magazine on how I broke my grumpy personality over my fiancée's sudden death.

To call it a day before I go home and let my housekeeper prepare my funeral clothes, I drive over to Raven. Five days ago, I was excited to tell her about Avène and my relationship progress. Now, I must mention the hardship along with it. I wanted to introduce Avène to Raven at least once, but it never happened.

CHAPTER 34
Nicholas

I ended up going back home last night at midnight because I had a lot to say to Raven. I didn't want to go back to an empty house, and I had the urge to feel Avène around me, so I stayed at her house for a couple of hours. Her scent, clothes, which I brought with me, and plushies all have memories of her and allowed me to feel she is still around me; it was comforting, allowing me to start the day today stronger than yesterday.

I started the day by picking up Alex from the hospital as he was discharged today. Before going home to get changed, I got his permission to come with me to check on the girls and pick up Denis and his nurse from the hospital. I want to take it slow and give Alex as much recovery time as he needs, so I promised myself that everything I want to do, I must take permission from him beforehand.

"Ready to experience what a house with six females and one male looks like?" I tease Alex before going into Anastasia's house, where the entire friend group and Cora's fiancé are gathered.

"How bad can it be?" I grin at his innocent answer because, last time, it wasn't that good of an experience. They are literal chatterboxes. I wonder how Caleb has been dealing with them.

"You'll see." He gets confused by my vague answer, so I ring the doorbell so he knows what I mean.

"Alex and Avène's attractive fiancée are here, guys!" Isabella answers the door, and Alex immediately side-eyes me.

"So, this is what you mean," Alex mutters when everyone comes around us, except for Anastasia.

"Okay, please give us personal space," I say when Caleb's body is literally sticking to my chest. "Where's Anastasia?" They all go silent.

"I'm here!" I hear her yelling from a distance. "Why are you so grumpy? Learn how to deal with body language. Otherwise, I'd feel bad for Avène," she jokes while coming towards us.

Everyone looks slightly brighter than yesterday for whatever reason. I don't ask what changed their moods so fast, but Alex reads my mind.

"Are you guys not sad Avène passed away? How can your moods be so bright?" he asks them straightforwardly. It could be the video that I had shown them of Avène's messages yesterday, but I didn't think it would make such a great impact.

"It's the video Nicholas showed all of us. It reminded us of how Avène would be scolding us if she saw us so distant from each other, crying over her death and killing ourselves with her," Anastasia replies after a couple of seconds of silence.

"From now on, let's get closer to each other like how Avène would want. Let's care for each other, create memories together, remember Avène together, and be happy for each other," Charlotte adds.

Anastasia keeps on staring at Alex, and she gradually makes her way to us and hugs him. "We're here for you," I hear her whisper in his ear.

"Okay, nice speech. We now must go and get Avène's brother and get ready. You should also get ready. Let's stop being emotional chatterboxes," I say to break the tense silence. We do need to get going; the funeral is in two hours.

"I told you so many times. Read the mood and stop being grumpy," Anastasia snaps at me.

"But we've got to go. No time for hugging," I smile at her, hold Alex's arm, and head towards the car, although they are all cursing out loud at me for not hugging any one of them, especially Isabella.

"Damn, never knew you had it in you to talk back to Anastasia," Alex says after he got over the shock of what he just experienced.

"I have it in me to do anything except talk back to your sister." When we are alone, I just refer to Avène as his sister since they were born only two months apart and have known each other since then. They even used to change each other's clothes as kids. Weird but typical of two sweet, caring siblings.

We pick up Denis and his nurse, and we head home. The housekeeper and Denis's nurse helped him get changed while Alex and I changed rooms alone. Alex always changes faster than me, so I go downstairs and find him talking to Denis. The sight is beautiful; they look like two normal brothers who have no burden or care in this world, making plans for their next hangout.

I let them be and go to the kitchen quietly, so Alex doesn't hear me while I pack his medication. Just because he looks like he is doing well, I won't take the risk, as his doctor advised.

Once I finished hiding the medication, I called Alex, Denis, and his nurse to get in the car before we get stuck in the traffic, since the funeral starts in 30 minutes. Anastasia and the others are on their way as well, as they informed Alex.

The goal for today is to have barely any tears cried over Avène, to let her rest in peace and to know that we are doing well. So far, that's going perfectly fine, but who knows how Alex or Anastasia might react when they see her grave.

The funeral went well, thank God. I was worried mostly about Alex, but he held through, and the same for Anastasia. Alex, Anastasia, and I did end up crying, but not as much as we have the past few days. I know for a fact that I only cried because I got that weird feeling again as I stared into Avène's grave, and it bothered me so much since I couldn't tell what it was. Otherwise, Denis did a great job; proud of him, and as a reward, I treated him to the finest chocolate cake to be found in Boston.

I left Alex with the girls and Caleb to go for dinner and spend the night together while I excused myself to go alone to the fields and spend the night talking to Avène through the stars. I kept on looking at the number of stars there are today compared to before, making the sky twinkle brighter than before.

I smiled when I felt that weird feeling again because I finally got what it was. This entire time, I hadn't realised that this feeling was mixed with sadness, happiness, love, guilt, longing, fear, and everything couples usually feel when planning for their future. Except that Avène and I's future isn't there, but there's a sky where we twinkle together.

I enjoy the silence, but as it gets late, I tell Avène what I have to say. "My love, I miss you. You were always the shining star in my life that shone even when I had my darkest days, but I never returned that shine until lately. I'm truly sorry, and as a thank you and to truly show my love for you, I have made a promise to myself that you'll forever be my first and last love, and I'll forever take care of Alex, Denis and the girls. They are having a fun recovery time right now, so don't worry, just rest in peace. I'll forever remember you even if the others forget you." I take a deep breath to help myself not get emotional again. "The last time I wrote a poem about you was the day I proposed to you, but today I would love to tell you a last one, especially since the sky is so bright with stars reminding me of the 'Twinkle, Twinkle, Little Star' song."

I stand up and look up at the sky to feel closer to it, compared to when sitting.

"Twinkle, twinkle, shining star,
Glowing from a world afar.
At night, your light is so bright,
Guiding us through your heart.
When you guide, warm, and wondrous,
Your story is calm and marvellous.
Twinkle, twinkle, gleaming light,
Spark our dreams with delight."

Epilogue

AFTER ONE YEAR

Tonight, Alex and Anastasia went on their first date, and I can't help but worry. Alex is immature, while Anastasia is slightly more mature than Alex; at least she swears properly instead of saying booger. They have been flirting with each other for an entire year, so Cora and I decided to push them and let them experience an actual relationship.

As for me, I have visited the field every other night. Alex and I would go to visit Avène's grave every Saturday since she was born on that day. The girls, Alex and Denis, would all gather at Avène's house once a month. I went back to work the week after the funeral before the media started to spread rumours. Now and then, I visit Elysium, and every weekend, I go to Raven unless work annoys me. Then, the pattern mixes up slightly.

Avène's graduation also took place two months ago, and she got recognised despite her passing. She could've been such a great sports journalist that I would've watched every single day, but unfortunately, life is unfair. Anastasia is the one who received Avène's degree since she's her best friend, so I also gave her the agreement to be the one to place it on Avène's memorial desk that we all set up together for her.

While staying in her house the other day, I came across the bucket list she had written. Seeing how much she had been able to tick off made me feel grief again. I saw the bullet point that said, "to publish my book," and I recalled the day she told me she was done with it, having only an epilogue left to write. So, I continued what she started and published it. She is getting recognised, and soon, the entire world will remember Avène Valikova.

Otherwise, I haven't heard from Sophia ever since the day she left home. I never visited Anderson's grave, but today I want to visit mother's as I miss her unconditionally. Avène always told me that I look tough on the outside but soft at my heart, and I fear I finally admit she is right. After an entire year of rollercoasters, I get it.

Overall, I care mostly about quality time instead of checking if I'm still a billionaire or if my competitors beat me. So far, NAVES is still the best-selling company, and my position is still the owner of the company, and I am still being referred to as a billionaire.

Eight months ago, I hated the way the company's name was my surname and created by Anderson, so I decided to change it to Naves, which symbolises my first name combined with Avène's initials. Other than that, my life didn't have a major life-changing event lately, unlike Cora and Caleb.

Cora and Caleb found out they were pregnant seven months ago, and two months ago they found out it's a girl. But out of respect and loyalty, they decided to do the wedding tomorrow until everyone has accepted Avène's death. So here I am, being forced by Isabella to wear my custom-tailored suit by Louis Vuitton, as shockingly I'm the man of honour.

Caleb and I have been becoming friends, but I swear I barely know that man well yet, and he chooses me to be the man of honour. When I asked him what the reason was, he said it was because I'm more mature than Alex. He was only able to choose between me and Alex since he had no other friends. The next reason why I accepted his choice, he said, is because Cora's maid of honour is Avène, even though she isn't with us anymore. Since she's my fiancée, he thought it would be wonderful to have two couples standing.

I agreed with him, and now I'm trying to put effort into it and am excited to be part of their new chapter. But the part I always, and will forever, look forward to more than any event is when I sleep at night, tasting dawn and hoping to find Avène shining her love at me alone the next morning.

THE ~~END~~

Thank you for taking the time to read *Everything Works Out In The End*. It makes me feel pleased to know this book has found its home. If you enjoyed this book, please consider leaving a review on your chosen platform(s).

Reviews help us authors more than you might think. I am forever grateful for every single one of them!

Love,

Marwa

If you can't get enough of Nicholas and Avène, visit my Instagram page so we can both fantasise about them! instagram.com/maarwaaaa

Acknowledgements

Like Avène, I also have a brother like Denis, a family friend like Alex, and a friend group like Avène's. I also had difficulties with my brother growing up, but I gradually learned how to love him, and everything worked out in the end. I hope all of you out there also learn how to love your loved ones before it's too late.

Avène and Nicholas are going to be my favourite characters forever, but it's okay if your favourite characters are Cora and Caleb or the others. Avène and Nicholas wouldn't have been brought to life without so many people around me, and I want to thank every one of them.

Notion Press has helped me make my dream become a reality. I cannot thank you or explain my appreciation just by words. I am truly grateful.

To whoever believed in me, thank you for putting up with my imagination and giving me the right motivation.

And finally, to the reviewers and readers who have shown this book so much love and honesty, I love you guys and will forever be grateful.

Looking out for the new book in everything works out in the end series...

FORBIDDEN
LOVE

She loved him but he loved her more..

Continue your *everything works out in the end* journey with Cora and Caleb's story.

www.ingramcontent.com/pod-product-compliance
Lightning Source LLC
LaVergne TN
LVHW091316150826
845673LV00006B/1664

* 9 7 9 8 8 9 5 4 4 5 4 6 4 *